A Robyn Hunter Mystery

You Can Run

Run

NORAH McCLINTOCK

D0123677

Scholastic Canada Ltd.
Toronto New York London Auckland Sydney
Mexico City New Delhi Hong Kong Buenos Aires

Scholastic Canada Ltd.
604 King Street West, Toronto, Ontario M5V 1E1, Canada

Scholastic Inc.
557 Broadway, New York, NY 10012, USA

Scholastic Australia Pty Limited
PO Box 579, Gosford, NSW 2250, Australia

Scholastic New Zealand Limited
Private Bag 94407, Greenmount, Auckland, New Zealand

Scholastic Ltd.
Euston House, 24 Eversholt Street,
London NW1 1DB, UK

Library and Archives Canada Cataloguing in Publication
McClintock, Norah
You can run / Norah McClintock.
(A Robyn Hunter mystery)
ISBN 0-439-95230-1
I. Title. II. Series.
PS8575.C62Y69 2006   jC813'.54   C2006-900580-X

Cover image by Renee Lee

6 5 4 3 2 1   Printed in Canada   06 07 08 09 10

To B.M.R., who really can run.

Chapter One

Ta-DA, Ta-DA, Ta-da-da-da-da-da-DA.

Morgan Turner, my best friend, looked at me. Then she looked at my backpack.

Ta-DA, Ta-DA, Ta-da-da-da-da-da-DA.

I ripped the pack off my shoulder as if it were on fire and dug through it until I found my cell phone.

"Hey, you know what that sounds like?" said Billy Royal, my other best friend.

"Yeah," Morgan said as I looked down at my caller ID. "It sounds like someone with very bad taste got their hands on Robyn's phone."

That someone was on the other end of the line now. I flipped open the phone.

"Hi, Dad," I said.

"Hey, Robbie. Just checking to see if the new phone is working okay."

"It's working fine, Dad."

"Great," he said. He sounded pleased. "Well then, I won't keep you."

"Okay. Bye, Dad."

"I know that tune," Billy said, frowning. Then his eyes lit up and he snapped his fingers. "It's *My Girl*, right?" He looked at me for confirmation. "Your phone plays *My Girl*. The Temptations, 1964, written by Smokey Robinson, right?" He nodded approvingly. "I love that old-time Motown sound." Billy was an oldies junkie. It was one of the reasons he got along well with my father.

Morgan looked at me, too, but the expression on her face was more along the lines of, *Tell me you're not that pathetic.*

"I lost my cell phone last week," I said.

"Moving up in the world, huh?" Morgan said. Until recently I had been famous for losing my house keys. Regularly.

"My mom got really mad about it," I said. My mother is famous for knowing the exact location of each and every one of her possessions — at all times. "Dad bailed me out. He bought me a new phone. He picked out the ring tone. He said it was perfect for me."

"It would be," Morgan said, "*if* you were his girl-friend instead of his daughter and *if* this were nine-teen-seventy-something."

"1964," Billy said.

"Whatever," Morgan said. "Take my advice, Robyn. Change it."

"But it's a *gift*," Billy said.

Morgan gave him an incredulous look. "It's a *ring tone.*"

"It's still a gift," Billy said.

"So?" Morgan said. "Didn't anyone ever give you a gift you didn't want?"

"Well, sure, but—"

"Maybe a sweater with reindeer on it from your granny at Christmas? Or a shirt that you'd never wear in a million years, not even at Halloween, from some old auntie who hasn't seen you since you were three years old?"

"Yeah, but—"

"So, when you get a gift like that, you exchange it for something you want, right?"

Billy looked down at his sneakers. Morgan shook her head in amazement.

"You're a nice guy," she said. Billy beamed. "But you can be such a wuss." Billy's smile evaporated like morning mist under a scorching sun.

I was stuffing my new phone back into my pack when Morgan suddenly tugged on my arm.

"Hey, Robyn, is that who I think it is?"

I looked around. "Who?" I said. Morgan, Billy and I had just come from the library downtown where we had been doing research for a project at school. We were going to get something to eat before heading home.

"Nick."

"Where?"

"Over there, with those kids. It sure looks like him."

She pointed to a bunch of kids who were clogging the sidewalk in front of a youth drop-in centre on the other side of the street. A couple of them were sitting cross-legged on the sidewalk with a hat upside-down in front of them, panhandling. The rest of them were crowding the sit-downs, making it impossible for pedestrians to get by, let alone drop coins into the hat. A couple of the boys were pushing each other around, acting like they were fighting, but laughing while they were doing it. I didn't see Nick.

"I don't think he'd be hanging around down here," I said.

"Right," Morgan said, her tone making it clear that she meant exactly the opposite. "Because if he were, he'd get busted."

Morgan had met Nick only once, but she loved to talk about him. She claimed to be intrigued by him. She said guys like Nick were "inherently fascinating." I think mostly what fascinated her was the scar that ran from the bridge of his nose to the lobe of his right ear. It made him look dangerous.

"I don't mean because he'd get busted," I said, although he would get into serious trouble. "I mean because he follows the rules."

"Right," Morgan said, still meaning exactly the opposite. "Following the rules is the best way I know to get arrested, not to mention end up in custody."

"It's *open* custody," I said. There were no locked cells, guard towers, or barbed wire where Nick was living.

"Open, closed, it's still custody," Morgan said.

She was right. And it was true. Nick hadn't always followed the rules. He'd been in a little trouble with the law. Okay, so maybe more than a little. But that was before. And he'd had his reasons. But he was doing better now. He was still living in a group home, serving out a disposition for, well, that was ancient history. Nick doesn't like to talk about it and I don't blame him. In another couple of weeks, his time would be up and he'd be out of there for good. There was no way he was going to mess that up by hanging out with a bunch of street kids downtown.

"Look, now you can see him," Morgan said. She grabbed my arm again. "It *is* Nick." She pointed at the group of kids sitting on the sidewalk and this time I saw him, with his thick dark hair and his typical Nick wardrobe — black jeans, black T-shirt, black jacket, black boots. I saw him, but I wished I hadn't. He had his arm around a girl. They were looking at something, but I couldn't see what.

"Which one is he?" Billy said. He had heard a lot about Nick, mostly from Morgan, but hadn't met him yet. While Morgan pointed him out, I stared. A sick lump formed in my stomach. What was he doing there? Why did he have his arm around that girl? Why was that girl leaning her head against his shoulder?

I turned my back to him before he could see me. I wanted to get out of there, fast. But Morgan had another idea.

"Nick," she called. She raised an arm and waved. "Hey, Nick, over here."

I *shhh*-ed her, but trying to *shhh* Morgan is like trying to *shhh* thunder. Once she gets started, she's a real force of nature. There's no stopping her. Morgan called Nick's name again. I ducked behind Billy, who is so tall and skinny that it was like trying to hide behind a length of rope. I peeked around him and saw Nick's head bob up in response to Morgan's call. He peered across the street at her as if he were trying to place her. Then he shifted his eyes a little to the right and saw me. He said something to the girl he was holding, then he let go of her and stood up.

"I want to go home," I said to Morgan.

"But it's Nick —"

"*Now*, Morgan." What was the matter with her? Didn't she see the girl he was with?

I turned and headed up the street, walking fast, not looking back. I had almost reached the subway station when someone grabbed my arm. I whirled around, angry now.

"Morgan, geeze —"

But it wasn't Morgan. It was Nick. He peered at me with his purple eyes. They were like two perfectly round pieces of amethyst. I had never seen eyes that colour before I met him.

"Hey, Robyn." His voice was warm and he smiled at me. He didn't look remotely dangerous now. "What's up?"

What's up? I had just seen him sitting on the sidewalk with his arm around another girl and he was asking *me* what's up?

"I'm in a hurry. I have to get home," I said. I glanced at Morgan and Billy, who were a few paces behind Nick. Morgan gave me a sympathetic look —

she'd finally figured out what was bothering me. Too bad it had taken her so long. Billy just shrugged, as if he couldn't understand what the big deal was, which, I guess, proves what Morgan is always saying: guys are blind, deaf and dumb when it comes to the nuances of relationships. Well, *most* guys are.

Nick seemed puzzled, probably by the chill in my voice and by the way I'd walked away when Morgan called his name. He looked at me for a few moments as if he were trying to work a complicated puzzle. Then he glanced back across the street at the group of kids he'd been with.

"Hey, you're not upset about Beej, are you?" he said.

The girl's name was Beej? What kind of name was that?

"Because there's no reason for you to be," he said. "She's just a friend."

Right. That explained why he'd been holding her in public.

"The guy she was going with took off. She's upset," he said. "I was just trying to cheer her up a little. She was showing me some of her pictures."

Uh-huh.

He stepped in close to me, put one hand under my chin and pushed it up a little, gently, so I had to look at him.

"It's not what you think," he said.

Maybe it was the warmth of his hand where he was touching me. Or maybe it was the sincere look in his eyes. Probably, though, it was the little lopsided smile he gave me — Nick hoping that I wasn't mad at him or, if I was, that I wouldn't stay that way.

"What are you doing down here anyway?" I said. "Aren't you supposed to be back at Somerset?" Somerset was the name of the group home where he lived. It was named after the street it was on, Somerset Avenue.

"I had to meet with someone at the youth centre." The way he said it, it came out casual, as if it were no big deal. But then he turned away slightly so that he wasn't looking at me any more, and I noticed a little twitch at the corner of his mouth. He gets that when something is bothering him.

"Is everything okay, Nick?"

"Sure." There it was, that twitch again. "I just had to see a counsellor, that's all. Mr. Jarvis is here with me. He's talking to someone inside. I'm just waiting for him." Ed Jarvis was Nick's youth worker. Then Nick smiled, but it came off looking forced, as if he were trying hard to keep the conversation light. "Come on," he said, taking my hand. "Come and say hi."

I turned to look at Morgan and Billy. Nick turned, too.

"Bring your friends along," he said.

Morgan shook her head. "Billy's going to collapse if he doesn't eat something in the next two minutes," she said. I glanced at Billy. He didn't look like hunger was going to get the better of him any time soon. He'd brought some snacks with him to the library and had spent at least half of his time in the cafeteria in the basement, eating them. Morgan knew that perfectly well because, as usual, she had commented on the vast quantities of food he was able to consume without gaining any weight. "We'll be at the Buddha," she said. "You can catch up with us there."

The Buddha was a vegan restaurant we went to a lot, mainly because Billy refused to eat anything that came from animals (or wear anything that contained animal products). Actually, in a funny way, it was thanks to Billy and his vegan-ness that I had met Nick.

I gave Morgan a grateful look and let Nick pull me across the street toward the knot of kids on the sidewalk.

The first thing I noticed was the piercings. I had never seen so many at one time. Almost every kid had something pierced — an eyebrow (or two), a nose, an earlobe (or two) as well as miscellaneous other parts of the ear, a lip (or two), a tongue, a belly button. Most of the kids had multiple piercings. A lot of them had weird hair — dyed, buzzed, spiked, dreaded. One boy and one girl had no hair at all. When Nick said, "Hey, everybody, this is Robyn," I felt like an alien who had just stepped out of a spaceship. The kids — especially the girls — stared at my Miss Sixty shoes and my Diesel jeans. They took note of my own modest piercings — one in each earlobe — and the small gold hoops with the pearls hanging from each one, another gift from my father. They checked out the earphones hooked around my neck that ran to the iPod that was visible in a mesh pocket in my backpack. Some of them gave me a curt nod of acknowledgement. Some gave me a hard look and then dismissed me. Not one of them said hello. I had never felt less welcome in my life, but Nick didn't seem to notice. He tugged my hand again and pulled me down onto the sidewalk. I hesitated. The sidewalk *looked* relatively clean, but when I thought about all the boots and shoes that had walked over it and where else they might have walked, I felt squeamish. It didn't seem to bother Nick, though, so I eased myself down beside him. He turned to the girl he'd had his arm around.

"Hey, Beej," he said. "This is Robyn."

Beej, I found out later, was short for B.J., but Nick said he didn't know what the initials stood for. Apparently she didn't like to say. Beej was a small, thin girl with five piercings in one ear, six in the other, and one in her left eyebrow. Her short hair was jet black, but I saw auburn at the roots. I smiled at her. She didn't smile back.

"Remember I told you about meeting Robyn at the animal shelter?" Nick said.

Beej said, yeah, she remembered. She stared at me as if she'd already made up her mind that she didn't like me and wanted to make sure I knew it. As she gave me the evil eye, one of the guys standing nearby called to Nick.

"Be right back," Nick said. He got up and went over to the guy.

Beej was holding a stack of photographs. When I tried to sneak a peek, she shuffled them together and slipped them into an envelope. Somewhere on the street someone whistled. Beej turned her head to check out where the sound had come from. I turned too, but couldn't figure out who had whistled. I saw a dog walker, with six big dogs, each one a different breed and all straining at their leashes, waiting for a light to change on the corner.

I glanced at Nick to see if he had noticed. Nick is crazy about dogs. But he was deep into conversation with a kid with a shaved head. Then I turned to Beej, who pointedly looked away from me. It was clear she wanted nothing to do with me. I sighed and looked around some more, as if I were new in town and the cityscape was fresh and fascinating instead of the same old same old — office towers, stores, restaurants, cars, buses, and pedestrians. I spotted someone I thought I recognized from school, a surly loner named Kenny. He was leaning against a utility pole on the other side of the street, scarfing down a street dog. When he finished it, he crumpled the paper napkin it had been wrapped in and threw it into the street — what a pig — and turned to walk away. If Morgan had seen what he'd done, she would have marched across the street, picked up the napkin, thrust it into his hand, and informed him, in case he didn't know, that littering was against the law.

I began to wish that Morgan and Billy had come with me after all. Then I wouldn't be sitting here awkwardly with Beej. I glanced at her again. She was tucking her pictures into a battered old backpack. She gave me a sharp look, as if by merely turning in her direction I was invading her personal space. I was relieved when Nick finally came back to where we were sitting and dropped down onto the sidewalk beside us.

"I told Robyn that you were showing me your pictures," he said to Beej. "I bet she'd like to see them."

And I bet Beej would rather have stuck a red-hot needle in her own eye than show them to me. Sure enough, instead of taking her pictures out again, she zipped her backpack and asked Nick for the time. When he told her, she said, "I gotta go. I'll see you around, Nick, okay?" She leaned over and kissed him on the cheek, looking at me as she did, maybe to see how I would react. I pretended that I didn't care. She got up, folded the blanket she'd been sitting on, slung her backpack over her shoulder, and walked away. A couple of other kids drifted away at the same time. I wanted to leave, too. I didn't feel comfortable there, not even with Nick beside me, holding my hand.

Then someone said, "Robyn?"

I looked up toward a surprised-sounding voice and saw Ed Jarvis, a stocky man with a brushcut. His deep voice, gruff attitude and stiff way of walking reminded me of a drill sergeant. He looked at my hand in Nick's. Then he glanced around, as if he were wondering where I had come from.

"Good to see you again, Robyn," he said. He took another look at my hand in Nick's. Nick must have noticed, too, because he squeezed my hand tighter and stared at Mr. Jarvis as if he were daring him to say something about it. "I've been meaning to call your father," Mr. Jarvis said. "He gave me some base-ball tickets last week. I took some of the kids. They had a terrific time." Like a lot of people, Mr. Jarvis knew my father. I told him I'd deliver the message. I also told him, because he asked, that school was going just fine. Then he said, "Time to go, Nick," and backed off a few paces.

Nick gave him a sour look, which told me that something was wrong. Nick usually got along well with Mr. Jarvis. He got up and helped me to my feet.

"How come you had to see a counsellor?" I said. "Is everything okay?"

His eyes shifted away from me again and for a moment his face went rigid, as if he were angry about something.

"It was just an appointment," he said. "It's not important." He pulled me close to him. "Three more weeks," he said. He didn't have to explain what he meant. I had been marking days off my calendar, too. In three more weeks, Nick's time at Somerset would be up and he could go to live with his aunt.

"Actually," I said, "it's two weeks and six days. But who's counting, right?"

"I am," Nick said. "It's two weeks and six days until I get out of Somerset. But it's exactly three weeks until your birthday."

I stared at him. "How did you—?"

He grinned. "You'd be surprised at what you can find out if you know who to ask," he said. He sounded just like my father. "You know what I'm going to do on your birthday?" His eyes sparkled.

"I'm going to take you out. First we're going to have dinner together somewhere nice. Then we're going to go to a movie. Unless you want to do something else — maybe see if anyone good is going to be in town, maybe go to a concert."

"A movie would be fine," I said.

"Then," Nick said, "I'm going to make sure you get home safely instead of having to leave you at a bus stop somewhere." Nick was allowed out of Somerset only with permission, never at night, and always with a strict curfew and restrictions on where he could go. A worried look flashed across his face. "Any chance you're going to be staying with your dad on your birthday?" Nick got along okay with my father. My mother, who is divorced from my father and with whom I live most of the time, made him nervous.

"Nick," Mr. Jarvis said, pointing at his watch. "Tick-tock."

He bent down a little and kissed me on the cheek. "Three weeks," he said. "It's gonna be great."

I watched him walk away with Mr. Jarvis and I wondered again about his appointment. Still, if he was going to be leaving Somerset on schedule, everything must be okay.

* * *

I don't remember walking from where Nick had left me to the Buddha. I was still thinking about him, still feeling his lips on my cheek. I spotted Billy first. He was sitting opposite Morgan with a puppyish look on his face that I had been noticing an awful lot lately.

I was beginning to think that he had developed more than friendly feelings for Morgan over the summer. She had been away at her family's cottage while he had been working in the city at a camp for young activists. Had her absence made his heart grow fonder? But as soon as I got inside, I knew I was wrong. They were arguing — well, actually, Morgan was giving Billy a hard time. Billy was his usual calm self.

As Morgan squished over to make room for me, she said, "I'm glad you're here. Now we can talk about something that someone actually cares about."

"What's going on?" I said.

"I was just wondering—" Billy began.

"No way," Morgan said. "I don't even want to hear her name. I told you yesterday that I didn't care. You've managed to make it through today without mentioning her. Let's keep it that way, okay, Billy? Besides, Robyn isn't interested in her either."

"Interested in who?" I said.

"Trisha Carnegie," Billy said.

Morgan scowled at him. "Didn't I just say that I didn't want to hear her name? Didn't I tell you that she was the last person we want to talk about or even think about? Isn't that right, Robyn?"

"Maybe she's the last thing *you* want to think about," Billy said. "But Robyn's interested, aren't you, Robyn?"

"I guess," I said. Actually, I wasn't interested in Trisha. But I didn't come right out and say so because Billy seemed to want to talk about her and I didn't want to hurt his feelings. Morgan, however, took a typical Morgan approach: she jabbed me in the ribs.

"Tell him," she said.

"Tell him what?"

"Tell him that you don't care about Trisha Carnegie."

"Well—" I began.

"See?" Morgan said. "Robyn doesn't care. I don't care. So can we *please* talk about something else?"

"You're putting words in Robyn's mouth," Billy protested. "Robyn is a sensitive person. She cares about the people around her."

Morgan gave him an irritated look. "*I'm* someone around her," she said. "*You're* someone around her. But Trisha Carnegie? Trisha Carnegie is *not* around her."

"Around *her?*" I said. "Hello? Am I invisible all of a sudden?"

Morgan ignored me. "In fact, Trisha Carnegie means nothing to Robyn."

That wasn't exactly true.

"Besides," Morgan said, "Trisha is *so* weird."

She wasn't the only person to hold that opinion. Everyone thought that Trisha was weird. She dressed funny — plaid skirts teamed up with knee socks and cardigans; capri pants and bowling shirt combinations; shirtwaist dresses, vintage 1955, paired with blazers. Some people could pull off a look like that. Not Trisha. Her crazy wardrobe only reinforced the weird way she acted. Her blond hair usually looked like someone who was either visually impaired or under the influence of serious medication had taken a weed-whacker to it. She had a row of safety pins stuck into one ear and a big metal stud stuck in the other — a look that was as retro as her wardrobe. Half the time she wore twelve-hole steel-toed boots, the rest of the time, ballet slippers. She always carried a genuine Dolce & Gabbana backpack, though, because, by the way, trash-dressing Trisha was a rich girl. And always, always around her neck was a chain from which hung a gold ring — her father's wedding band — and a little leather pouch containing a chunk of crystal.

Trisha wasn't a friend of mine. I don't think she was anyone's friend. She didn't hang out with any group or any person that I knew of. She barely talked in class. Sure, she had to do presentations like the rest of us, but she always picked out-there topics. Last year, in Western Civilization Up to the Fifteenth Century, she did a show-and-tell on the history of torture. Her poetry presentation in English was on — who else? — Sylvia Plath. In World Issues, she enlightened us all about the globalization of disease, including a gruesomely detailed account of the progress of the Ebola virus through the human body. Very dark — that was Trisha.

Kids who had gone to elementary school with Trisha swore that she hadn't always been so weird. One kid I knew even insisted that she had been perfectly normal up until she was twelve years old. That was when she had completely freaked out. Apparently she had never freaked back in again. The story I had heard went like this: Trisha and her father had gone on a camping trip together. It had been a real wilderness trip. They canoed and portaged their way through the backcountry, just the two of them, I don't even know how many kilometres from civilization. Then one night when they were sitting around a campfire, her father had a heart attack. Trisha wanted to help him. She knew it all depended on her. But she was twelve years old and out in the wilds. What could she do? Someone said her father had taken a cell phone on the trip but Trisha couldn't get a signal. Someone else — I don't remember who — said that Trisha had tried to get her father into the canoe. Her plan: to paddle him and portage him however many kilometres back to where they had started. Maybe she would get lucky along the way. Maybe she would come across another camper. Maybe she would hit the jackpot and run into a doctor who was out camping with his family or maybe with some doctor buddies.

But Trisha's father was in no shape to walk and she was too small to carry him. She dragged him a little way, but she couldn't get him into the canoe.

He died.

Someone said he died while Trisha was signalling SOS into the darkness with a flashlight. Someone else said he died with Trisha screaming for help into an empty night on an island who knows how far from another living soul. Everyone who told the story said that Trisha had screamed herself silent by morning when a canoe with two teenage boys in it happened by. Trisha got their attention by throwing rocks at them from the shore. But by then it was too late for the boys to do anything but tell her to stay calm — and try to stay calm themselves — while they went and got somebody. Somebody to take the body out. From what I'd heard, Trisha had been in serious therapy after that. Some people said she still was.

Two years later — or, as someone who had known Trisha at the time put it, two *short* years later — Trisha's mother had remarried. Some people said the guy she married was a real jerk. Other people said he was okay. Everybody agreed that Trisha had never forgiven her mother for replacing her father. This was supposedly why she wore her father's wedding ring around her neck, to let her mother and her stepfather know that, as far as she was concerned, she had only one father. She had even worn the ring to the wedding.

These days, Trisha could be seen talking to a chunk of crystal. I had no idea what that was all about — maybe she was into new age meditation. All I know is that I'd see her at lunchtime or between classes or even sometimes when she was supposed to be in class, sitting cross-legged at the end of some hall, caressing the crystal and muttering to herself.

"Bonkers," is how Morgan summed up Trisha. "I mean, come on, you don't need to be a psychiatrist to figure that out." Morgan's mother was a psychiatrist. "Whoever her shrink is, he should lose his license. I mean, all those years of therapy and Trisha just gets crazier and crazier."

Nobody I knew disagreed with that assessment — not even me, although, unlike Morgan, I had a few other, more complicated, feelings about Trisha.

I looked across the table at Billy, and said, "Okay, I give up. Why are you so interested in Trisha all of a sudden? What did she do?" As far as I knew, Billy didn't know Trisha any better than I did. I had never seen him talk to her. She wasn't in any of his classes, except for homeroom.

Billy stared at me as if I had just reappeared suddenly after a couple of years on a desert island. "Didn't you hear the announcement at school yesterday?" he said.

I shook my head. Every morning while our homeroom teachers took attendance, we were subjected to a barrage of announcements from the school office — only five thousand tickets left for the school dance this Friday; anyone who wants to participate in the car wash to raise money for the school band should sign up on the sheets in the band room; the next chess club meeting will be held Tuesday at lunch. Stupid stuff that hardly anyone listened to. Besides, yesterday morning in homeroom, I'd had earphones on and had been listening to a recording I had made. I was scheduled to give a speech in my second period Urban Geography class. I had recorded it and kept playing it over and over. It was the best way I knew to learn a speech. So, no, I hadn't heard and no one had mentioned it to me, probably because I had left school right after my speech. My French class had taken in a French film downtown.

"Trisha made an announcement?" I said. "About what?"

"She didn't *make* an announcement," Billy said. "The announcement was *about* her. She's missing."

"What do you mean, missing?" I said. Sure, Trisha was weird and annoying. But missing? That didn't sound good.

"I mean, no one knows where she is," Billy said. "Supposedly she's been missing since *Wednesday*. Mr. Elton" —our school principal— "read a note from her mother asking anyone who knows where she might be to please contact her."

Since Wednesday?

Morgan rolled her eyes again. "That is *so* typical," she said.

"What is?" Billy said.

"It's axiomatic," Morgan said. "The weirder the kid, the less likely the parents are to realize that she has no friends and that probably nobody even notices, much less cares, that she hasn't turned up at school."

The pathetically adoring look that had been in Billy's eyes changed to one of shocked disapproval.

"You're talking about another human being," he said.

Morgan looked sternly at him. "Really?" she said. She was more selective than Billy about which sentient beings she included in her personal universe. "Did *you* notice she wasn't there before the announcement?"

Billy reluctantly admitted that he hadn't.

"I rest my case," Morgan said. She turned to me. "Look on the bright side, huh, Robyn? Maybe she's gone for good. If she is, you definitely won't have to do another project with her."

"You know what?" I said. "Let's change the subject." Because, boy, if there was one thing I didn't want to think about, it was Trisha Carnegie.

Morgan cheerfully changed the subject — to herself — and that, I thought, was that.

I was wrong.

Chapter Two

Mostly I live with my mother, but I spend every other weekend at my father's place and I drop by to see him whenever I feel like it or whenever I'm in the neighbourhood. This was my father's weekend, although you wouldn't know it based on how much I had actually seen him. He wasn't home when I got back after my Saturday afternoon at the library with Morgan and Billy and he still hadn't returned by the time I went to bed, although he did call to tell me not to wait up for him. He was gone again when I rolled out of bed around noon on Sunday morning. I did some homework, went for a late-afternoon run in the park, and came back to his still-empty loft. He must have come in while I was in the shower because after I had dried my hair and changed, I found him sitting in the living room. He had a file folder open on his lap, but he was staring out the window, thinking. He kept right on thinking, even when I asked him a question — twice.

So I tried a new question. "Big case, huh, Dad?" My father used to be a cop. Now he has his own private security company. He does a booming business, which, if you ask me, doesn't say much about the state of the world.

He nodded distractedly. Whatever he was thinking about, he seemed to be deeply immersed in it, which was just like him. I doubted he'd heard anything I had said. I repeated my earlier question for a third time. To my own ears, I sounded a lot like an American tourist asking for directions in Tibet: I was talking far too loudly and slowly, as if the person I was talking to had very little grasp of the language I was speaking. Sure enough, my usually alert father seemed to catch only one word.

"Birthday?" he said. A look of alarm appeared in his eyes. "Is it your birthday already?"

"Relax, Dad," I said. "You haven't missed it yet. It's still three weeks away."

His face flooded with relief and he flashed me his trademark Mac Hunter grin, the one my mother said she used to think of as boyishly handsome and that had made her weaken, as she put it, in the first place.

"I can't believe my baby's going to be sixteen," he said, shaking his head. "Why, I remember the day you were born as if it were yesterday."

"That's not the way I heard it," I said. The story my mother told was that my father had been working on a big case when she went into labour. He had promised her he'd get to the hospital and he did. A day late.

He shrugged. "Okay," he said, "so maybe I remember the day *after* you were born a little better." My father has an *a-guy's-got-to-do-what-a-guy's-got-to-do* attitude to his work. It still drives my mother crazy, although she has to be more careful about complaining now. A few years before my parents separated, my mother had gone back to school. She's a lawyer now and puts in long hours at the office, which means that, like my father, she isn't always able to get home when she promised.

"So, is it okay, Dad? Can I spend my birthday here this year?"

My father lost the faraway look in his eyes and focused in hard on me. "Won't your mother have something planned?"

"She hasn't mentioned anything," I said, even though I knew that she would probably want to take me out to dinner to celebrate. My mother is very big on special occasions.

"The whole time I've been living here," my father said, "you've never spent your birthday with me." He peered harder at me. "So what gives?"

I looked right back at him and tried to decide whether he would blab my reason to my mother if I told him. But I didn't have a chance to make that decision because the intercom buzzer sounded. My father occupies the entire third floor of what used to be a carpet factory. He owns the whole building, too, which makes him the landlord for a popular gourmet restaurant on the ground floor and half a dozen apartments on the second floor. He could easily live on what he makes from rent, but my father isn't the kind of guy who could ever be happy sitting around cashing rent cheques.

"Get that for me, would you, Robbie?" he said. "It's probably Vern."

I crossed to the door, pressed the button on the wall and said hello into the speaker, expecting that the answering voice would be that of Vernon Deloitte, another ex-cop and my father's business partner. Instead, I heard a voice that I didn't recognize.

"Hello?" it said. "My name is Carl Hanover. I'm looking for MacKenzie Hunter."

It amounted to a total of eleven words, but they got my father's attention in a way that I hadn't managed to. He set aside the file folder he had been holding, got up, and strode across an expanse of hardwood floor to the door. His thumb replaced mine on the button.

"Carl, is that really you?" he said into the speaker.

"Mac? Thank goodness," the voice said. "I need to talk to you."

"Come on up. I'm on the third floor," my father said. He pressed a second button, the red one that releases the lock down on the first floor. Then he stepped out into the hall to wait. A few moments later, I heard footsteps on the concrete steps that led up to the third floor.

I stood in the doorway, wondering who Carl was and why my father had sounded so surprised to hear his voice. I watched my father step back a pace from the top of the stairs to allow his visitor up. When he said Carl's name again, the surprise in his voice was still there, as if he couldn't believe his good fortune. They hugged each other. It was quite a sight, two big men embracing like long-lost brothers.

"My God, how long has it been?" my father said, pulling back to look at his old friend. "Ten years?"

"More like thirteen or fourteen," Carl said. He was a good-looking man who either spent a lot of time down south or was completely oblivious to the hazards of tanning machines. He had a deep, rich tan. "As I recall, the last time I saw you, you were singing the blues about the terrible twos." He looked around my father at me. "This must be Robyn."

My father turned and beamed at me. "She's a real chip off the old block," he said. "Robbie, this is Carl Hanover. We've known each other since—"

"Since forever," Carl said. He slapped my father on the back. "We went to school together."

My father urged Carl to come in. He offered him something to drink — beer, coffee, bottled water. Carl said thanks but he was fine. They sat in the living room area while I retreated to the kitchen to make myself a cup of tea. When it was ready, I perched on a stool at the counter that divided the kitchen from the dining room to drink it. I had a newspaper open in front of me, but because my father's loft is almost entirely open concept (the only completely private spaces are the bathrooms, the two bedrooms, and a room that my father calls his office), I could see my father and Carl Hanover and hear every word they were saying.

At first it was catch-up stuff. My father asked about the ten years Carl had spent out west. Different pace out there, Carl said. Slower. Then Carl wanted to know how Patricia, my mother, was. Great, my father said. By the way, we're divorced. Carl said that was too bad. He said, "I heard you have your own business now, I've been hearing all about you and your dirty tricks."

Dirty tricks? I glanced at my father, who shook his head and said he didn't think he would go so far as to call them dirty.

"But they are tricks," Carl said. "I heard one story about a woman who hired you to find her ex-husband and her kids. You tracked the guy to Mexico, right?"

"Right," my father said.

"The way I heard it, you sent someone into his house, supposedly to work as a maid, and *she* kidnapped the kids from him and you spirited them back here. I heard the guy actually called the cops." Carl laughed at that. He said, "That was borderline illegal, but that's never bothered you, has it, Mac? The end justifies the means, right?"

My father replied that the guy had given up custody of the kids, that he'd never paid a dime in child support, but that when his ex-wife wanted to remarry, he'd decided to punish her by taking the kids. All my father had done, he said, was make things right. Then he said, "How's the insurance business treating you?"

Carl said, "I can't complain, although I haven't spent much time in the office lately." My father said he had heard about Howie Maritz and asked if Carl happened to know him. Carl said, no, he'd met him professionally a couple of times, that was all, and he couldn't imagine what would drive a man to do something like that. (I wondered idly who Howie Maritz was and what he'd been driven to do.) Then my father caught Carl off guard by asking him how fatherhood was working out for him.

"Technically, it's stepfatherhood," Carl said. "How did you know about that?"

I peeked up and saw my father shrug, but I know he loves it when people ask him that question, usually in an awestruck tone of voice. He prides himself on knowing all kinds of things and loves to ambush people with his knowledge.

"So, how is stepfatherhood?" my father amended.

"Only about a million times harder than I ever imagined it could be," Carl said. "My stepdaughter is, well . . . let's just say she's a challenging kid. Volatile. Temperamental. I'd be lying if I said we hit if off immediately. We didn't. Even though we've managed to find some common ground, she still drives me crazy sometimes. But the hardest thing to put up with is the way she treats her mother." He shook his head. "Denise's first husband died under tragic circumstances. Of course the girl was devastated. I understand that. She was very close to her father, so I get that she wasn't exactly thrilled when Denise started seeing me. But we got along at least on some level — that is, until Denise and I decided to get married."

"She didn't take it well?" my father said.

"It's been nearly two years and she still hasn't forgiven her mother. If you ask me, she goes out of her way to punish Denise."

"Must be rough," my father said. "Maybe things will improve as she gets older." Carl didn't look convinced. "So, what made you decide to look me up after all of these years?"

Carl slumped in his chair. He said, "Well, that's the thing, Mac. She's the reason I'm here. My stepdaughter."

"What's the problem?"

"She's gone," Carl said.

"Gone?"

"Ran away. We have no idea where she is."

"How long has she been gone?"

"She went to school Wednesday morning. We haven't seen her since."

I glanced over at Carl Hanover. *Wednesday?* Talk about a coincidence.

My father frowned. "That's five days. Have you contacted the police?"

"When she didn't show up or call by the end of the week, Denise called them — not that it will do much good. The thing is, Mac . . ." He hesitated and gave my father a sorrowful, almost beaten, look. "This isn't the first time she's run away. She does it whenever she's upset about something or whenever she's angry with her mother. The first time, the cops found her within twenty-four hours and brought her back home." He shook his head. "I thought they were going to arrest Denise and me. You wouldn't believe the crazy stories that girl told the police about how she was mistreated at home. It was terrible. The child welfare authorities got involved. We were cleared, of course."

"That must have been a nightmare," my father said.

"You don't know the half of it. The next couple of times she ran away, Denise insisted on calling the police, but I have to tell you, every time I was afraid what the police would think. Since then, well, I guess a chronic runaway isn't high priority for the police. We've mostly just waited her out."

"And she's always come back?" my father said.

"Yes. It's always the same — she makes us sweat it out for one night, occasionally two. She always calls after the first night. Always. She calls and she and Denise talk. If all goes well, they have a good cry over the phone, and then she comes home. If it doesn't go well, she's gone for another night. But she always comes home."

"If she's been gone since Wednesday morning, then she's been gone a lot longer than usual," my father said. He studied his old friend. I had a pretty good idea what he was thinking: Why is this time different? "What happened, Carl? What set her off?"

"To be honest, I'm not entirely sure," Carl said. "I know she was upset about Denise, but it could have been something else, too. It's hard to tell, Mac."

"And you're worried?"

"We both are. When she still wasn't home by Friday morning, Denise called the school, you know, to see if she was at least attending classes. She even asked them to put the word out to students."

Called the school? Put the word out?

"I drove around downtown all day Friday and again yesterday to see if I could spot her. While I was out, Denise called the police."

"You don't suspect foul play, do you, Carl?"

Carl hesitated. "The police asked Denise the same thing." He stared down at my father's coffee table. Finally he shook his head. "No," he said. "No, we don't suspect foul play. But there are all kinds of people out there — you know that, Mac — and, like you said, this is the longest she's been gone and so far she hasn't called home even once. We haven't heard a word."

"What did the police say?"

"That they'd keep an eye open. But they also know her history. They said that she's sixteen, which means that she can live wherever she wants. They also said that girls that age are complicated. According to Denise, the police officer she spoke to said, 'maybe she has issues.' Geeze, *I* have issues. My stepdaughter has run away and all we get from the cops is, 'be patient.' They said, she's done this before and she's always come home, right? They said, she'll probably call; she'll probably be home in another day or two. If she's done this before, she knows what she's doing. They said, maybe she's at a friend's house."

"Have you checked with her friends?" my father said.

"She doesn't have any that we know of," Carl said. He seemed embarrassed to have to admit it. "What kind of sixteen-year-old girl doesn't have any friends?"

I glanced at my father, who was still sitting forward in his chair, his elbows resting on his knees. He shrugged as if he had no idea how to answer the question. I did, though. I knew exactly what kind of girl he was talking about.

"Denise is afraid that Trisha's gone for good this time," Carl said.

And there it was. *Trisha*. Carl Hanover's stepdaughter was named Trisha. That clinched it — what were the chances that *two* 16-year-old loners named Trisha had run away last Wednesday?

"Why would Denise think that?" my father said.

Carl sounded utterly defeated as he said, "Denise is sick. Cancer. This is her second bout with it, Mac, and it doesn't look good. Denise thinks that's why she ran. Trisha was traumatized by her father's death. She was in therapy for years. She took it really hard the first time Denise was sick. We were afraid she was going to have a complete breakdown. Now Denise is sick again and she thinks that Trisha has run away so that she won't have to go through another death, she won't have to face being abandoned by her only other parent. Denise always feels responsible when Trisha runs away. She feels more responsible this time, even though it's not her fault that she's sick. She's worried about how Trisha is handling her illness."

Trisha's mother has *cancer*? If only I had known.

"I told her it could have been something else that set Trisha off this time. Maybe something happened at school. She's an odd kid, Mac. I don't think school is easy for her. Maybe that's why she ran. If things were different, I'd say let her go. Let her try to fend for herself out there for a week or two. Maybe it would help straighten her out and make her grateful for what she has. Maybe she'd appreciate her mother more and be more compassionate. But with Denise the way she is . . . Maybe Trisha really does resent her for being sick or maybe she's afraid of being abandoned, I don't know. All I know is that Denise *needs* Trisha back. She needs to know she's safe. I thought maybe you could help."

"You want *me* to try to find her?" my father said.

"You do that kind of work, don't you? I'll pay you. Please, Mac. The police said if they see her, they'll approach her. But if she's managed to stay out of sight for this long, that could mean she's gotten smart about ducking the cops. Or that she's found someplace to really lay low. I've driven all over the city and I've got nothing. All I need is a lead on her whereabouts, and I can take it from there. I won't pretend that Trisha and I always see eye to eye, but I'm pretty sure that if I could just talk to her and find out what the problem is, I could make her see how much she's hurting her mother. I love Denise, Mac. I can't stand to see her so worried, not in her condition."

My father was silent for a moment. He was probably thinking it over, balancing an old friend's request against whatever jobs he was already working on. Finally he said, "Let's not worry about that right now. Why don't you tell me a little more about Trisha?"

When Carl said what school Trisha went to, my

father glanced at me. There was no way he didn't notice the look on my face.

* * *

"Since when do we chase down runaway kids who don't want to be found in the first place?" Vernon Deloitte said about an hour later — after Carl Hanover had left my father's place, after my father had made a phone call to the police officer Mrs. Hanover had talked to, and after we had rushed downstairs to where Vern had been waiting for nearly half an hour. "And what about this Doig thing? I thought we were going to take that one."

The three of us were sitting in La Folie, the restaurant on the ground floor of my father's building. We were having supper before my mother came to pick me up. My father had just told Vern what he'd agreed to do. Vern seemed less than thrilled.

"Teenage girls are always running away," he said. "Who can even guess what they're thinking half the time? If you ask me, they're the real mystery of the universe."

I cleared my throat. Vern glanced at me. His face reddened a little and he mumbled, "Present company excepted, of course."

"The girl who's missing is Carl Hanover's step-daughter," my father said. And, wait a second, what was that look Vern gave him? And what was that look that my father gave Vern in return? "He's worried about her. Anyway, it'll probably turn out just like the police said — she'll show up at home in another day or two."

"Carl Hanover," Vern said. He glanced at me again. "Your old friend Carl Hanover, the insurance adjuster?"

My father nodded.

"You think it's related?" Vern said.

"Related to what?" I said.

"No, I don't," my father said to Vern. "I checked with Cecile." Cecile, the police officer Mrs. Hanover had spoken to about Trisha. "She's got a record of four runaways for this kid over the past eighteen months, and those are just the ones her mother reported. Apparently when Denise Hanover called the police this time, she told them that Trisha has run away maybe a dozen times. Whenever the girl gets upset or angry with her mother, she takes off."

"Related to what?" I said again.

"Nothing important," my father said.

I could have pressed them for an answer, but my father and Vern are ex-police officers. That means they're both one hundred percent committed to not talking about their work with outsiders, which, to a cop, includes everybody who doesn't carry a badge and a gun. I'm used to it. My mother is just as bad. She's a criminal lawyer. She doesn't open up much about what her day at the office, or court, was like, either. But that doesn't mean I'm completely clueless. They meant related to the "Doig thing" Vern had mentioned. I'd read about Carmine Doig in the newspaper. He was a millionaire horse breeder who was rumoured to have some unsavoury acquaintances. A couple of months ago, there had been a fire at his stables. A man and several horses had died. The fire had been ruled accidental. But if my father and Vern were interested in what had happened, there was more to it than what I had read in the paper. "We're going to take the Doig job," my father said. "But I'm going to look into this, too. Carl's an old friend."

Vern still didn't look happy, but he said okay and pulled a small notebook out of his jacket pocket. "I'm out there as much as you are. I can keep an eye open, ask a few questions. Give me a rundown on Trisha Hanover."

"Actually," my father said, "she goes by the name Trisha Carnegie. She kept her father's name when her mother remarried. Isn't that right, Robbie?"

Vern looked across the table at me, one eyebrow raised.

"She goes to my school," I explained.

"So you know her?" Vern said. My father watched me a little too intently.

"Not really," I said.

"But you've seen her around, right?" Vern said. "You probably know who she hangs out with."

I shook my head.

My father studied me. "You might be surprised what you know about someone you think you don't know," he said.

I said maybe. What I was thinking was: my father would have been surprised how little he knew about someone he thought he knew extremely well.

Like me.

Chapter Three

I was pretty sure my father was going to start asking me about Trisha Carnegie when, thank you, thank you, *thank you*, I was saved the bell. My father's cell phone rang. He pulled it out of his pocket, checked the display, and smiled an all-too-familiar smile.

"Patti," he said fondly.

I checked my watch and was surprised at how late it was. My mother should have picked me up ages ago. The way it usually happened: she called me when she was leaving the house (or her office) to tell me she was on her way. When she arrived, she stayed outside in her car and called me on my cell phone to tell me she was waiting for me. But today she hadn't called me. Instead, she'd called my father. That had to mean that something was wrong.

Uh-oh. I pulled out my cell phone. There was one new message.

As a result of Morgan's teasing me about the ring tone my father had chosen for me, I had put my phone on vibrate. That wouldn't have been a problem if I had remembered that I'd done it and if my cell phone had been in my pocket instead of in my backpack, which was on the floor at my feet. As it was, I didn't notice when it vibrated. That meant that my mother had no choice but to try to reach me first on my father's home phone and then, when that didn't work, on his cell phone. Usually she tries to have as little direct contact with him as possible, not because she hates him or anything but because, despite being divorced, he still acts like he has a shot at winning her back. I don't know if he really believes that or if he just acts that way to drive her crazy. If it's the latter, he's doing a terrific job.

"Your mother is waiting for you outside," my father said when he finished his call. "She is *not* happy."

I shut my phone off, threw it in my backpack, wriggled into my jacket, and hurried for the door. My father was right behind me when I got to the curb where my mother was pacing. She looked stern and lawyerly, even on a Sunday evening, in navy blue slacks and a pale blue blouse, her hair pulled back, her blue eyes focused on me, her mouth turned down in annoyance. She said she'd been worried when I didn't answer my phone. When I lied and told her that I'd switched it off (I didn't want to hurt my father's feelings), she scolded me. But, if you ask me, the real reason she was annoyed was that my father was leaning against her car, grinning idiotically at her.

"You're absolutely right," he said, which seemed to catch my mother off guard. She stared at him as if he had just apologized for every meal he had ever missed while they were married, every anniversary he had ever forgotten (which, according to my mother, was most of them), and every Christmas that he'd left all the shopping up to her. She told me later that she had been in shock because she couldn't recall him ever saying those exact three words to her before.

"That was inconsiderate of Robbie," my father said. "I'm sure she's sorry for worrying you, aren't you, Robbie? We got a late start on supper and Robbie lost track of the time. Isn't that right, Robbie?"

"*You're* wearing a watch, Mac," my mother pointed out. "And you know I always call Robyn before I leave the house. Didn't you think that maybe something was wrong?"

"You're absolutely right," he said again. "I should have paid more attention to the time myself."

My mother eyed him suspiciously, as if she suspected that he was trying to hide something from her. Finally she said, "Get in the car, Robyn." She started for the driver's side.

"Wait a minute, Patti," my father said.

"Patricia," my mother corrected. She hates to be called Patti. She says it makes her sound as if she's five years old. My father, on the other hand, loves the name Patti. He loves it so much that he persists in using it despite my mother's preferences.

"You remember Carl Hanover?" my father said. "You met him a few times when Robbie was a baby."

My mother nodded. She still had a suspicious look on her face.

"He came to see me today. His stepdaughter is missing. He wants me to help him find her. The girl goes to Robbie's school. I thought we could all go upstairs for a few minutes and I could ask Robbie some questions—"

I tensed up at the thought of my father grilling me. My mother tensed up at the thought of entering my father's loft. She had never set foot in it.

"Forget it, Mac," she said.

"But, Patti, a girl is missing."

"Does Carl think she's in danger?" she said.

"No," my father admitted. "She's run away before. But he *is* worried."

My mother turned to me. "Do you know this girl, Robyn?"

"Not really. She's in one of my classes, but she's not a friend or anything."

"Do you have any idea where she is?"

"No." And that was the truth, so help me.

My mother looked at my father. "I don't see how Robyn is going to be able to help you," she said. "Shouldn't you be concentrating on the girl's friends?"

"But—"

"Get in the car, Robyn."

I climbed obediently into the passenger seat. It took all of two minutes from the time we pulled away from the curb in front of La Folie for my mother's cell phone to ring. She pulled over and answered it. She listened for a moment. Then she said, "I am not her receptionist," and hung up. She glanced at me.

"Do me a favour, Robyn," she said. "Turn on your phone."

I did. My phone rang — well, it played *My Girl*— almost immediately. My mother shook her head as she pulled back into traffic. I held my phone to my ear.

"Hi, Dad."

"She's mad at me, huh?" he said.

"You have to ask?"

"Call me when you get home, okay? I want to talk to you."

"What about?" I said, as if I didn't already know.

"Please, Robbie?"

"It's late, Dad. I haven't finished my homework."

My mother shot me a disapproving glance.

"It won't take long," my father said. He hung up.

"Well," my mother said, "what does he want now?"

"Nothing important."

My mother didn't push the point. In fact, she didn't say anything at all, which wasn't normal. My mother has always taken a big interest in my life. Before she went to law school, she took so much of an interest in every detail of every day of my life that Morgan used to tease me about it. Morgan's mother was much better than my mother at separation, according to Morgan. Morgan's mother felt no need to live vicariously through Morgan the way Morgan thought my mother did with me, at least until she started law school. Then, I guess because she felt bad about being away so much and having to bury herself in her books when she was home, she put aside what she called 'talk time' — time to discuss my day. It's a regular part of life now. If she's home for supper, we talk while we cook and while we eat (but never with our mouths full; my mother has a rule against that). If she isn't home for supper, we talk when she gets home. If I've been staying with my father, we talk when she picks me up. *Always*. But not this time.

"Is everything okay, Mom?"

"Everything is fine," she said.

Then why didn't it *feel* fine? Not only was my mother uncharacteristically quiet, but she seemed preoccupied.

"Did you see Ted this weekend?"

Ted Gold is the man my mother has been seeing. He's a financial analyst. I'm not one hundred percent sure what a financial analyst does, but I know that Ted is good at it and that he's made a lot of money. He isn't one of those flashy rich guys, though. He dresses down more than he dresses up. He loves to cook, especially for my mother. He also loves to listen to jazz, although he's flexible. He volunteers as a basketball coach one night a week at a youth centre not far from where my father lives. He never misses a game. And even though he's a short, balding, nerdy-looking guy, all the kids seem to like and respect him. I like him, too.

"I worked all weekend," my mother said.

"Even on Saturday night?" No matter how busy she was, my mother usually reserved Saturday nights for Ted.

"I had an important case dropped on me at the last minute."

I didn't doubt that. But something was wrong. I was sure of it. Except for Saturday when he was with my mother, Ted usually called her every night. But, I realized now, he hadn't called her at all last week, at least, not that I had noticed.

"Did you and Ted have a fight or something?" I said.

"What makes you think that?"

"He hasn't been over to the house in a while."

"Scheduling problems," she said. "It's been hectic." Hectic?

"You were home every night last week," I said.

"I mean *his* schedule has been hectic," she said.

"Since when is Ted ever too busy to see you?"

That's when my mother did something that she always claims she tries to avoid. She got angry with me. "For heaven's sake, Robyn, stop giving me the third degree," she said. This was followed by something she always claimed she would never say: "You sound just like your father." Believe me, it wasn't intended as a compliment.

"Thanks a lot," I said. If she didn't want to talk to me, fine. After what she'd just said, I didn't want to talk to her, either.

It was quiet in the car. I stared out the passenger side window.

"Robyn?" my mother said after we had gone a few more kilometres.

I continued to stare out the window.

"Honey, I'm sorry. I shouldn't have said that. It's just that—"

I turned and saw a troubled expression on her face.

"Ted and I are taking a little break, okay?"

I said okay, even though the look on my mother's face told me that it was not okay. I wondered whose idea the "little break" had been. I wondered if it would turn out to be permanent. Most of all, I wondered how my mother was feeling about it, whether she was hurt or angry or confused or all of the above. But she didn't volunteer to tell me, so I didn't ask. She was quiet the rest of the way home. It wasn't until we pulled into the driveway and she opened the garage door with her remote that she finally reverted to standard mom mode.

"Didn't you promise me that you would clean out the garage?" she said as she nudged the car inside.

Yes, I had promised — right after my mother had *ordered* me to clean it out. But talk about a Herculean task. I'd have traded the Augean stables for my mother's garage any day. Ask almost anyone and they'll tell you that my mother is a neat freak. She keeps the house in impeccable order. A lot of times, though, she accomplishes this by piling stuff willy-nilly in the garage.

"I'll do it, honest," I said.

"When?"

I hate being put on the spot, especially when a miserable, thankless chore is involved.

"Probably next weekend."

"*Probably?*" my mother said. "Make that definitely, Robyn."

Right.

When we got inside, my mother headed straight upstairs. She said it had been a gruelling day and that there was nothing like a long Sunday in the office preparing for court to make a person want to soak in a hot bath — forever. I went into the kitchen and stared at the telephone for a few minutes. I didn't want to call my father. I knew what he wanted to talk about, and I didn't want to talk about it. But if I didn't call him, he would call me. He would keep calling until he got hold of me and by then he would know for sure that something was wrong. It was probably better to get it over with. I picked up the receiver, punched in his phone number, and spent the next few minutes telling him everything — well, almost everything — I knew, had ever heard, and was willing to admit about Trisha Carnegie. It didn't take long.

"Do you have any idea who she would confide in, Robbie?"

"No, Dad."

"Who does she talk to at school?"

"I already told you. No one."

"Everyone talks to *someone*, Robbie. You can't spend five days a week in a building with fourteen hundred other human beings and not talk to any of them."

It was obvious that my father had been out of high school for a very long time. "Yes, you can, Dad. You can also spend five days a week in a building with fourteen hundred other human beings and have *them* not talk to you."

There was a brief silence on the other end of the phone.

"So you're saying that this girl not only has no friends, she has no acquaintances either, no one she might talk to regularly?"

"If she does, I don't know who they are."

"What about teachers?"

"What about them?"

"Is she close to any of her teachers?"

"I don't know, Dad."

"It's just not possible that no one knows anything about this girl," he said.

"I worked on a project with her and *I* don't know anything about her," I said. There, it was out in the open. Now nobody could rat me out.

"What do you mean, you worked on a project with her?"

"In history," I said. "I told you. She's in my history class."

"She didn't mention anything about what was going on in her life?"

"No."

"She didn't mention any names to you, people she might know, places where she hangs out?"

"No."

"She didn't mention her mother?"

"No." I was glad I was talking to him on the phone and not in person. If he had seen my face, he would have known that I wasn't being completely honest with him. He would probably see a few other things, too. "Dad, for the millionth time, she doesn't talk much." She didn't work much, either, which had been my number one problem with her.

"Well, thanks, Robbie," he said at last.

"Sorry I couldn't be more helpful," I said. Then, mostly to change the subject, I said, "Dad? I forgot to tell you. I saw Mr. Jarvis yesterday. He said the baseball tickets worked out great — the kids he took had a good time."

My father said he was glad. Then he said, "Where'd you see him, Robbie? Don't tell me you were protesting again." He was referring to my scrape with the law in the summer, the one that had ended with an agreement that I volunteer at an animal shelter in return for a storeowner not pressing charges against me. Long story.

"Very funny, Dad. I ran into him downtown. Nick was with him."

"Oh?" That was all he said, but there was something about the sound of that one syllable — cautious? guarded? — that caught me like a whiff of smoke. And where there's smoke . . .

"Did he say anything to you, Dad?"

"Who?"

"Mr. Jarvis. Did he say anything to you about Nick when you gave him those tickets?"

"Like what?"

"That's what I'm asking."

"Not that I recall. Why?"

48

I knew then that there was something he wasn't telling me. For one thing, his voice was pitched a little higher than normal. For another, he was answering my questions with more questions, a sure sign of evasion. It probably served me right.

"So Mr. Jarvis *didn't* say anything to you about Nick?"

"No," my father said. Then, after a tiny pause, he said, "Your mother looked a little out of sorts when she picked you up. Is she okay?"

One more thing to hide.

"She's fine, Dad."

After I hung up, I couldn't shake the feeling that something was going on with Nick, maybe something to do with his appointment, and that my father had an idea what it was.

Chapter Four

"Geeze, slow down for a second," Morgan said. "Where's the fire?"

She had caught up with me at my locker, where I was cramming textbooks and binders from my last two classes into my locker as fast as I could.

"I'm going to see Nick," I said. Our school works on a two-day cycle. On Day One, I have a full load of classes. On Day Two, I have a spare right before lunch, which gives me enough time to get across town to meet Nick at his school if I want to. This was a Day Two and I wanted to.

"Oh?" Morgan said, grinning. "And are you going to come back with that same goofy expression on your face that you had on Saturday?"

"Goofy?" I said.

"As in, crazy in love," Morgan said. "He's really hot, Robyn. What are his friends like?"

"Nick kind of keeps to himself," I said. I jammed my math textbook onto the already tightly packed top shelf of my locker and slammed the door. "Gotta run," I said.

I had to wait almost fifteen minutes for a bus that was supposed to come every five. Then the bus hit every red light between my school and my destination. By the time I got to Nick's school — a small, extremely alternative, school located above a sporting goods store in the west end — Nick's lunch period had already started. I knew that because one of the teachers, a fifty-something guy in jeans, with his greying hair in a ponytail and a stud in one earlobe, told me when I reached the top of the stairs. When I asked him if he knew where Nick was, he shrugged and said, "As long as they're back by one o'clock, it's all good with me."

I scouted the fast food outlets in the vicinity and finally found Nick in the back of a taco place, scarfing down an order of nachos as if he hadn't eaten all day, which, knowing Nick, he probably hadn't. The way he told it, the staff at Somerset have to drag him out of bed every morning and even then, he said, it's a miracle he gets to school on time most days. He is not, as he puts it, a morning person. He glanced up and saw me coming toward him, but he didn't do what I had hoped he would. He didn't smile. He didn't even look pleased. Instead, he reached for the jacket that was hooked on the back of his chair and he pulled it on over his T-shirt. When I reached his table, he stood up and kissed me on the cheek. I was confused, but the kiss made me feel better.

"You had me worried for a minute," I said. "I

thought you were going to run out the back door."
When he looked baffled, I explained. "As soon as you
saw me, you put on your jacket."

"It's kind of chilly in here," he said.

It wasn't.

"You want something to eat?" he said,

I didn't.

"Nick, is everything okay?"

"Sure," he said. But instead of looking at me, he
looked down at what was left of his nachos. He stared
at them for a long time, as if all those bits of taco chip,
sour cream, black olives and cheese were infinitely
more fascinating than me.

"Nick?"

His head bobbed up and he smiled at me. The first
time I had seen that smile, it had felt like a miracle.
Most of the time Nick looks like a tough guy, dressed
all in black, tall for sixteen, and lean, and when he's
serious or angry, you don't doubt that he could do a
lot of damage. He'd been in trouble for most of his
life.

"You sure you don't want something to eat?" he
said. "How about something to drink?" He jumped to
his feet before I could answer.

"Nick, I—"

But he was already striding to the counter at the
front of the restaurant. I watched him study the menu
items on the wall above the cash register. He spoke to
a girl behind the counter. When he came back, he
handed me a soda. I noticed he used his right hand.
Nick is left-handed.

"Diet, right?" he said.

"Right."

He sat down again, pushed aside his paper plate, and bent over his own drink. His face was pink and there were beads of sweat on his upper lip.

"It's warm in here, huh?" I said.

He nodded, but instead of taking off his jacket, he stood up again.

"Come on," he said. "I'll walk you to the bus."

The bus? I'd only just arrived, and now it sounded like he wanted to get rid of me. I thought about Beej. He'd had his arm around her, but right after that he had kissed me and told me that he wanted to take me out on my birthday. I thought about how he had acted when I asked him what he was doing downtown with Mr. Jarvis and how he'd acted just now, when I'd walked into the restaurant. What was going on?

As soon as we got outside, he peered up the street, cupping a hand over his eyes to block the glare of the autumn sun.

"I think I see your bus," he said.

"I have plenty of time."

"Yeah, but I have to get back. I have to study for a test." He started for the bus stop, then stopped and gestured to me. "Come on," he said. "You're gonna miss it."

I didn't. I reached the bus stop at the same time as the bus. Before I climbed in, I said, "How about Wednesday? I could come over here again. I'll get here earlier."

Nick shook his head. "I'm busy on Wednesday," he said. "Another time, okay?" But he didn't say when.

* * *

I had met Nick less than two months ago, when we were both volunteering, well, *sort of* volunteering, at a local animal shelter. I liked him — *a lot* — and sometimes I was one hundred percent positive that he liked me, too. At other times, though, like when I was on that bus, I wasn't so sure. Nick can be hard to read. My mother represented him the last time he was in trouble, and she doesn't really approve of me being involved with him. It isn't that she doesn't like him. In a way, I think she does. But she thinks I'd be better off with a regular guy, in other words, someone who hasn't been in youth court half a dozen times and who isn't serving a disposition in open custody. I think that's why I went to my father's place after school instead of my mother's.

My father was sitting in the living room again when I got there. He was hunched over his coffee table, which was buried in paper — newspaper clippings, printed documents, handwritten notes. He barely looked up when I let myself in. When he did finally glance at me, he seemed distracted. "Oh, hi, Robbie," he said. "How was your day?"

"Okay, I guess." He didn't pick up on my lack of enthusiasm, which was fine with me. I didn't much feel like talking. "I'm going to do my homework."

I went into the bedroom that my father calls my room, but which I know for a fact he treats more like a guest room. People from out of town stay in it sometimes. So do old friends, clients who need a place to stay, and Vern some nights when he and my father have been working late.

I closed the door and flung myself onto the bed. It's probably nothing, I told myself. Nick probably just has something on his mind, that's all. People are allowed to have things on their mind, things that they don't necessarily want to tell other people. Besides, it wasn't as if he was my official boyfriend. We liked each other, but maybe he liked other people, too. I told myself it was no big deal. But that wasn't true.

Every now and then I'd catch myself daydreaming: Nick and me, walking somewhere nice, maybe down by the pond in the park, or maybe strolling in one of the ravines that cut through the city, or maybe even outside of the city completely. It would be spring, when the wildflowers are in bloom and the air is fragrant with shower-soaked earth and moss and pine, when you swear you can smell each blade of grass, each bud on each tree. And there we'd be, just the two of us, maybe holding hands, maybe sitting on a blanket by a creek with the sun glinting off of it, eating a picnic lunch and talking. Talking about anything and everything. Or maybe not talking at all. When you're really comfortable with a person, you don't need words — or so I've heard. Yeah, I know. It sounds like a Hallmark moment. If it had been someone else's daydream, I would have laughed. But that's how he made me feel. ·

But what had happened today wasn't anything like my daydreams. Instead of being comfortable with me, Nick had acted nervous, jumping up and down, pretending he was doing things for me, when really he was just staying busy so he wouldn't have to talk to me. He hadn't been overjoyed to see me, that was for sure, and he had wasted no time getting rid of me.

I lay on the bed, thinking about Nick instead of my homework, until my stomach began to growl. I'd skipped lunch and now I was starving. I got up and went to see what my father had planned for supper.

He seemed startled to see me.

"You remembered I was here, right, Dad?"

He nodded, but I was willing to bet he hadn't.

"Aren't you hungry?" I said.

"Does your mother know you're here?"

Oops.

"Call her and tell her I'll make sure you get home. Then we'll go downstairs and get a bite to eat."

I did and then we did. We were both preoccupied and at least one of us knew it. Unless someone made a stab at conversation, it was going to be a dreary supper. So after we settled into our booth in La Folie, and after we had ordered, I said, "You were really lost in thought, Dad. Is everything okay?"

"Everything's fine," he said.

"It's that job Vern mentioned last night, isn't it?" I said.

My father nodded. Just then, the waiter arrived with our food. My father looked down at his plate and smiled appreciatively. La Folie is his favourite restaurant. Mine, too. The food is always terrific, even when all you have is a turkey-and-tomato sandwich and an order of fries, which is what I'd ordered. The chef used thick homemade bread, which he toasted, and real turkey — no Wonder Bread or processed turkey slices. And the fries were *frites* — thin and crispy and served with a little cup of mayonnaise. It was heaven.

My father cut into a chicken breast coated with Dijon mustard and crushed pecans.

"You heard about that fire a couple of months back?" he said. "Five horses died, along with a trainer at a stable north of the city."

"Carmine Doig's place, you mean?" I said. When my father looked surprised, I said, "I can read, Dad. It was in the paper. But I thought it was an accident."

"That's what the fire marshal's report says." He sounded as if he wasn't convinced.

"Did you talk to the fire marshal?" I said.

"I can't. He's dead. Suicide. They found him last Tuesday morning in his garage."

Oh.

"I read his report, though. He didn't find any evidence of arson. He concluded that the trainer was overcome by smoke. Apparently he had an office inside the stables. The theory is that he'd been celebrating a little too enthusiastically after a race and was overcome by smoke before he could wake up."

The *theory?* It sounded as though my hunch last night had been right. "Is that what you're doing, Dad? Looking into the trainer's death?"

"Carmine Doig calls himself a businessman," he said. "He's a developer. Made a fortune putting up office buildings north of the city. Now he's into subdivisions and horses. Race horses. But the company he keeps . . . it's not nice, if you know what I mean."

"So you think the trainer's death wasn't an accident?" I said.

"I don't think anything yet," my father said. "I'm just looking into things."

"Because someone hired you to?"

"The trainer's sister." He took another couple of bites of chicken. "It doesn't add up," he said. "Everybody has somebody in their life."

Huh?

My father looked casually across the table at me.

"You know what else I did today, Robbie?"

I said I didn't.

"I went back to school. Specifically, I went to *your* school. I talked to kids, teachers, the principal and the vice-principals, even the school secretaries."

I tried to look interested. I tried not to look guilty.

"And all I came up with is that one of the secretaries *thinks* she saw Trisha arrive at school on Wednesday morning. But she obviously didn't make it to homeroom because her homeroom teacher marked her absent. In fact, all of her teachers said she was absent that day and all of them said they had no idea why she wasn't at school. All except one." He looked directly at me. "You want to know which one?"

He didn't have to tell me. I already knew. I looked down at what was left of my supper. When I looked up again, I said, "Dad, I have to tell you something."

Chapter Five

I blame it all on my substitute history teacher. If you ask me, they should put leashes on substitute teachers. At the very least, they should lay down one clear law that all substitute teachers *must* follow — or else: Don't rock the boat.

Before Ms Twill, my history (Sixteenth Century to the Dawn of the New Millennium) teacher, had to leave town unexpectedly (and for an unspecified length of time) to care for her sick father, she assigned us our first major project of the year — an essay and presentation. Okay, fine, no problem. I've been in school long enough to know that major projects are part of the game. So I chose my topic — the Reformation — and made a note to start my research. Then, when it turned out that Ms Twill was going to be away for longer than anyone had expected, Ms Lewington, her substitute, decided that we should do the assignment in pairs. She assigned partners based on who was working on what topic. I got paired with — who else? — Trisha Carnegie.

"You know what that's all about, right?" Morgan had said when I told her.

"Yeah. Bad karma."

Morgan shook her head. "Laziness," she said. "Think about it. This way, Ms Lewington has half the number of essays to mark and half the number of pre-sentations to sit through."

"The presentations have to be twice as long as Ms Twill told us, because there are two of us," I said.

"There you go," Morgan said. "That way they'll take up as much class time as they originally would have, so Ms Lewington won't have to do any extra teaching."

Morgan had a point, but I wouldn't have cared one way or the other if I hadn't been stuck with Trisha.

At first I adopted what would universally be acknowledged as a positive attitude. I've worked with partners before. I've been stuck in groups of three or four people, each with wildly different per-sonalities and work styles. I've also been assigned to groups in which I was the only person who did any work, which means that I've simultaneously felt the pride of getting an *A*-plus *and* the bitterness of having to share that *A*-plus with a couple or more slackers. That's the reason I prefer to fly solo rather than as part of a flock. But in this case, I decided to be a big girl and get on with it.

I maintained my resolve until it became obvious that not only was Trisha weird but that she also had no interest in history (at least not between the sixteenth century and the dawn of the new millennium) and no apparent intention of doing her fair share of the work or, as far as I could see, any work at all.

The two-week anniversary of me being stuck with — I mean, *paired* with — Trisha coincided exactly with the two-week anniversary of her doing *absolutely nothing* in the way of reading or research on our topic. By then I'd developed what could only be described as a bad attitude, the kind that if my mother ever got wind of, she would have been disappointed in me as only a mother could be. But I couldn't stand it anymore. I decided to take action. I went to Ms Lewington and told her that if it was all the same to her, I would prefer to work alone.

It wasn't all the same to her.

"What did I tell you?" Morgan said. "No way is she going to let you create more work for her."

"How would separating us make more work for her?" I said. "In case you weren't listening, Trisha isn't doing *anything*."

Even if Morgan was right — and maybe she was — Ms Lewington would never have let on that her response was in any way a workload issue. Instead, she spun it into a 'real-world learning experience' issue, as in, "In the real world, you have to work with all kinds of people" — here she paused to consult her seating plan for my name (Morgan: "See? She hasn't even made an effort to learn anyone's name!") — "Robyn, is it?" Ms Lewington said.

I said it was.

She smiled at me in that way teachers do when

they are satisfied in their hearts that you are wrong and they intend to let you know precisely how.

"The modern workplace has embraced the team concept," she said. "Disparate groups of people, each with their own strengths and, *er*, areas needing improvement" — in other words, weaknesses — "team up to produce results that no single team member could produce on his or her own."

"But, see, that's the problem," I said.

She kept smiling; her lips looked as if they were frozen in place.

"The marking for this assignment includes a team component," she said. "I advise you to work it out."

I tried. I really did. The next day Trisha and I got together, during class — Ms Lewington was very generous about letting us use class time to work on our assignments. She even let us go to the library to do research. (Morgan: "That way, she cuts down not only on her teaching time, but on her preparation time, too." I was beginning to see a deeply cynical side to Morgan.)

"So," I said to Trisha, "let's see your notes."

Trisha did what Trisha would have been awarded a gold medal for if it were an Olympic sport — she stared down at her desk.

"We're supposed to be a team, Trisha," I said as patiently as I could, which, truthfully, was not all that patient. "Teamwork implies two or more people working together toward a common goal," I said. "In this case, that means—"

"I'm sorry," she said.

It was nice of her to say so. It would have been nicer if I hadn't heard it a few dozen times already.

"Trisha," I said, "when we divided up the work" — actually, *I* had divided up the work because, as I've already mentioned, I had done *everything* so far — "I thought we agreed that we would share it equally. But so far—"

"I'll go to the library right now," she said. She got up and left the classroom.

Well, okay.

I gathered my things and headed for the library, too. I admit it, I was curious. Was Trisha actually (finally) going to work on our assignment?

When I got to the library, she wasn't there. Of course, that didn't mean that she wasn't working somewhere else. And, to be fair, she hadn't explicitly said that she was going to the *school* library. For all I knew, she could be in the local library, maybe even the main library downtown, beavering away on the assignment. If you're going to dream, dream big, right?

Trisha didn't show up for the next three classes. I found her in the second-floor hall on Tuesday — *last* Tuesday, the day before we were supposed to do our presentation in front of the whole class. I hadn't been looking for her, but she was impossible not to notice. She was sitting cross-legged on the floor in front of a bank of lockers, her eyes closed, her crystal in her hand. I only noticed her because some kids near me — niners, I think — were pointing and giggling. Trisha was talking to herself.

I looked at her. I considered my options. Then I walked down the hall, stood in front of her, and said her name. And got no answer.

So I said her name louder.

She raised her eyes and tipped her head back to look at me.

"We present tomorrow right after homeroom," I said.

Boy, if there was a thought, any thought at all, reflected in those blank eyes of hers, I sure didn't see it.

"Trisha—"

"I did the work," she said. "I did what you said."

If I knew Trisha — and I had at least some insight into her by then — it was probably too little. It was definitely too late.

"We have to present tomorrow—"

"I'll bring my stuff," she said. "I'll meet you here at eight o'clock, before school starts."

Don't ask me why, but I said okay. I'd like to say that I said it because I believed her. I'd like to pretend that at that moment I saw all the good in Trisha, that I thought she'd seen the light, and that I knew in my heart she wouldn't let me down. I'd also like to say that I didn't go home and stay up all night doing both my work *and* hers. I'd like to say that I didn't plan to show up at school and hand her part of the presentation to her and tell her, *just read it, okay?* I'd like to say all of those things, but none of them would be true. I did not go to school the next morning filled with confidence that Trisha would be there, have all her work done, her half of the presentation rehearsed, and that she'd be ready — even eager — to show me her stuff.

I was there at eight o'clock.

She wasn't.

She wasn't there at eight-oh-five or eight-ten either. Nor was she there at eight-fifteen or eight-twenty or eight-thirty.

The first bell — the warning bell, the five-minutes-to-homeroom bell — rang at eight-forty-five, or approximately the same time that Trisha appeared in a plaid skirt and a pilly green cardigan, her face as white as milk.

"I'm sorry," she said.

"Forget it," I said.

"No, really, I'm sorry," she said.

"No, really, forget it," I said.

"It's my mother," she said.

Right. Her mother.

"She's sick," she said.

Uh-huh. Well, I figured I had to give her points for being slightly (marginally, fractionally) more creative than "the dog ate my homework."

"Whatever," I said because I was so angry that it was all I could trust myself to say.

"I did the work. I can show you," she said. She pulled off her D&G backpack and started to rummage through it and — guess what? Her pale face became paler. Her small eyes that only looked big because of the thick eyeliner she used grew wide. And she said (all together now . . .) "Oh my god —"

"Forgot to pack your part of the presentation, huh?" I said.

She stared at me. She even managed to make her eyes water.

"I'm—"

I held up my hand to silence her. I did not want to hear one more lame apology.

"I'm so tired. I was up all night. My mother's really sick and—"

That's when I said what I'd been hating myself for ever since, maybe the meanest thing I've ever said, maybe — and this was what had been eating at me since last night — the thing that had sent her running.

I said, "I don't care." I said, "Nobody cares." I said, "Maybe if you weren't so weird, people *would* care, but they don't."

She stared at me, a stunned expression on her face.

"I did the work," she said. "I just forgot . . . I'll go and get it."

"Trisha? Never mind, okay? *I* did the work. All of it. All you have to do is show up and read what I wrote for you. You think you can do that? Or is that too much for you to handle?"

The final bell rang. I shook my head and turned away from her. Boy, was I mad. I had done every last scrap of work. I had produced an *A*-plus project for sure, and Trisha was going to get the same mark even though all she'd done was coast. Life can be so unfair.

I went to homeroom. Then I went to history class.

Trisha did not show up.

I did the presentation alone. Before I began Ms

Lewington said, "Where's your partner, um" —
finger on the seating plan again — "Trisha?" When I
said I didn't know, Ms Lewington grunted with what
I can only assume was disapproval — as if it were my
fault that Trisha hadn't shown up, as if I had failed to
"work it out" with Trisha, as Ms Lewington had told
me to, and now I was going to lose marks for the
"team component." Which is why I did what I did
next. I lied. I told Ms Lewington that when I said I
wasn't sure where Trisha was, I meant that I wasn't
sure if she was at home or at the doctor.

"You mean she's sick?" Ms Lewington said.

I told her, yes, that's what I meant. I also told her
that Trisha had given me her part of the assignment
and that I was going to present it for her. In retro-
spect, it made me feel a little better. But like Trisha's
work, it was too little, too late.

Chapter Six

"In other words," my father said when I had finished my confession, "you're afraid it's *your* fault she ran away."

I nodded.

"You're being too hard on yourself, Robbie. Maybe she didn't do her work because of what was *really* bothering her, and what was really bothering her is what made her run away. Maybe it has nothing to do with you at all."

Maybe. Not a comforting word under the circumstances.

"Still, I could have been — *should* have been — nicer to her, especially when she told me her mother was sick."

My father didn't argue with that. Instead he looked at me with his grey eyes. I have the same eyes, the colour of slate. "So," he said, "it looks like you were the last person at school to see her."

I nodded. I wasn't proud of myself.

"You saw her, the bell rang, you went to home-room, then you went to your history class, but she didn't show up. Right?"

"Right," I said.

My father took a few more bites of his supper. Then he said, "You know a kid named Kenneth Merchant?"

"I know who he is," I said. A stringy kid with chewed-up fingernails and, as far as I could tell, a semi-permanent scowl on his face. He had transferred to my school partway through the final semester of last year. I sort of knew him — everyone sort of knew him. He was the kind of person who kept the rumour mill grinding. Everyone had heard at least one story about where he had been before he transferred to our school — every place from a juvenile detention facility to a boot camp to a psychiatric hospital to living on the street — and why he had been there. All of the stories were sketchy on details, so it was hard to tell which of them, if any, were true. I had never spoken to him, and he had never spoken to me. But what did he have to do with anything?

"Did you ever see him with Trisha?"

"I've never seen him with anyone. He isn't in any of my classes. Why?"

"I got the impression that he knows Trisha."

"Got the impression?"

"One of the teachers mentioned seeing them together a couple of times." Oh? "She remembers because she was surprised — two loners, is how she described them."

"Did you talk to him?"

"I tried to. But he wouldn't open his mouth. Wouldn't look me in the eye, either. Just shook his head a lot."

"You think he knows something about Trisha?"

"That's what I'd like to find out." He fiddled with his coffee, stirring it even though it was half-finished and probably lukewarm. "You know, in a situation like this, normally what I'd do is send in an investigator." Maybe like he'd sent in that woman who had gone undercover as a maid to grab back the two kidnapped kids. "Someone young enough to pass for a student. Have them go in, establish a presence, ask around, see what they can find out."

"Normally?"

His smoky grey eyes hadn't left mine for a second.

"First of all, it's hard to find someone who can pass for fifteen or sixteen. Second—" He paused for a heartbeat — why the hesitation? "You're already there, Robbie. People either know you or have seen you around. You're part of the landscape." Somehow that didn't sound flattering. It was like being compared to wallpaper. Or floor tile. "And," he said, "from what I've been able to gather, people don't make an automatic connection between you and me."

That was probably because, as far as I knew, he had never set foot in my high school — until today, that is.

"You want me to talk to Kenny?" I said.

"He might say something to you that he wouldn't say to me." He raised a hand to catch the waiter's attention. "But maybe you don't want to mention it to your mother," he said.

"Sure."

He reached across the table and put one of his hands over mine.

"I would never ask you to do anything if I thought it was dangerous or would get you in trouble. You know that, right?"

I knew.

"Carl Hanover is an old friend. And you're already there."

"Dad, it's no big deal. I'm happy to help." And I was, too. Maybe it would ease my conscience because, despite what my father had said, I still felt partly responsible for Trisha running away.

He squeezed my hand. "Come on. Let's get you home."

We zipped home in Dad's black Porsche with the sound system blaring vintage rock 'n' roll. My father had just bought AC/DC's greatest hits and played it at ear-splitting volume all the way. My mother would not have approved. She's more of an ABBA or Celine Dion kind of person. Personally, I'm more on my father's wavelength.

* * *

My mother was coming out the side door when we pulled into the driveway. She had a bulging green garbage bag in one hand, which she dropped into a trash can. She turned and looked at my father's Porsche. He switched off the engine.

"Dad," I said. I gave him a pleading look. What I

really meant was, *Don't*. Don't get out of the car. Don't try to go into the house. Don't bug Mom. Don't do anything that will annoy her, like flashing her a boyish grin or trying to give her a little peck on the cheek. But I don't think he heard me. He flung open the car door and stepped out onto the driveway. I hurried out the passenger side.

My father grinned at my mother. He's always delighted to see her. My mother generally doesn't share his enthusiasm.

"Patti," he said, "you look fabulous. As usual."

I waited for her to correct him the way she does every time he calls her anything but Patricia. I waited for her to cross her arms over her chest and give him her stern warning look. I waited for her to thank him for driving me home, using that tone of voice that told him, forget it, your charm doesn't work on me.

She did none of those things. Instead, she looked at him with blue eyes that seemed warm, even affectionate, although I knew I must be misreading her. She said, "Hi, Mac." She looked at him, really *looked* at him, instead of dismissing him the way she usually does. She gazed at him for so long that I checked him out, too, to see if she was seeing something that I hadn't noticed. But no, it was the same old Mac Hunter — a tall guy with thick dark hair speckled with just a touch of grey. A good-looking guy, even I could see that, with dimples when he grinned. A guy who was fit and trim for his age. There was no paunch on my father: he worked out at the gym four or five times a week and ran 10K regularly. He dressed well, too, although today he was just wearing blue jeans and a T-shirt under a black leather jacket. Women were always looking him over, checking out the third finger of his left hand for a wedding band, which, of course, he didn't wear.

My father reacted to my mother's non-frigid greeting the same way that I did. His grin slipped a little. He took a step toward her. When she didn't retreat or tell him to back off, his expression grew serious.

"Is everything okay, Patti?" he said.

She shook her head, not to say no, but as if she were coming out of some kind of daydream.

"Of course," she said. "Why wouldn't it be?" She looked at me. "Do you have homework, Robyn?" I nodded. "Then you'd better come in and do it. It's getting late." She looked at my father again. "Goodnight, Mac," she said. She walked up the path to the front door and went inside.

My father turned to me. "What's going on with your mother?"

"Nothing as far as I know," I said. I tried to sound as if I meant it. My mother would never have forgiven me if I'd told him about her and Ted's little break from each other. "Long day, I guess."

My father stared up at the house. "I know she doesn't like you to talk about her with me," he said. "But if something's wrong, if she needs help, *anything*, tell her—" He stopped and turned to me. "Tell her she can count on me. She can ask me for anything, no strings attached. Okay, Robbie?"

I told him okay. He stood in the driveway a little longer, leaning toward the house like a flower leaning toward the sun. Then he got back in the car, revved the engine, and backed down the driveway.

Chapter Seven

Some days I go with the flow. *Que sera sera.* What will be, will be. Don't fight it. Let it happen. Whatever.

Other days I have a plan. Goals. Objectives. Today was one of those days. Today I was going to do the favour that I had promised my father. I was going to find out what, if anything, Kenny Merchant knew about Trisha Carnegie. Specifically, I was going to find out if he knew where she was or why she had run away. My father was most interested in the former. I wanted the answer to the latter because, no matter what my father had said, I couldn't shake the feeling that I was the straw that had broken the camel's back, that I was the one who had pushed her into running. If I'd been nicer to her, if I'd been understanding when she'd said her mother was sick, if I'd bothered to ask what was wrong with her mother, if I'd thought for a moment about how I would have felt if I were in her situation, then maybe she wouldn't have taken off and maybe her (poor sick) mother wouldn't be so worried.

The way I had it mapped out, it would go something like this: I would say, "Hi, Kenny, Trisha's in my history class, we were doing a project together and, well, we had a little misunderstanding. (See? I was ready, willing, and able to take some responsibility.) I need to talk to her, it's important, so do you have any idea where I could find her?" And he would say . . . well, I wasn't sure what he would say. But I was hoping it would be something helpful.

The way it actually happened:

"Geeze, Robyn, couldn't you have grabbed us some seats?" Morgan said. She came toward me carrying a tray loaded with a bowl of vegetarian chili, a slice of whole grain bread, a bottle of apple juice, and her wallet. I was standing just inside the cafeteria door, where I had been looking for Kenny Merchant. I'd spotted him, too. He was in the food line, three people away from the cash.

"Here, hold this for a minute, will you?" Morgan said. She thrust the tray at me, picked up her wallet, and started to tuck it into the mini backpack she uses as a purse. "See if you can spot a couple of empty chairs," she said as she pulled out a mirror. Kenny was one person away from the cash now. Morgan looked into the mirror and made a face. "A zit," she said. "I can't believe it. I cleanse every morning and every night, and I'm getting a zit." Kenny was at the cash now, paying for a plastic-wrapped submarine sandwich. Then he moved past the cash and looped around, heading back toward the door.

"Morgan—"

"How come I never see *you* with a zit?" she said. She made it sound like I must have made a pact with the devil.

"Morgan, here, take this," I said. I shoved the tray at her and turned away without checking to see if she had a grip on it. I heard a gasp and then a crash. Morgan cursed and called my name. But I was already out of the cafeteria, running after Kenny.

He wasn't especially tall for a guy, but he had a long stride. He was halfway down the hall before I caught sight of him again. He was gone altogether by the time I reached the spot where I had seen him.

"You, Hunter," someone called. Mr. Dormer, one of the vice principals. "No running in the hall."

I skidded to a halt, muttered an apology, and started speed walking.

By the time I'd got to the exit door at the end of the hall and pushed it open, Kenny had vanished. I scanned the schoolyard. There were kids dotted and knotted all over it, but none of them was Kenny. It was so frustrating. I'd almost had him back in the cafeteria. Now, because he wasn't in any of my classes, I was unlikely to run into him during the afternoon. I could try to catch him after school, but there were half a dozen exits from the building and I had no idea which one he would use, which meant that I had a much better than even chance of missing him.

Then fortune smiled on me.

As I turned to go back inside, I spotted him. He was at the top of the bleachers that ran along one side of the athletic field.

I crossed the field and started to make my way to where he was sitting, working his way methodically through the sandwich he had bought in the cafeteria. He heard me coming and looked down at me as I climbed toward him. I smiled, to show that I was friendly and to put him in a relaxed mood. He stared back at me and took another bite of his sandwich. He chewed with his mouth partly open.

When I got close enough, I said, "Hi."

He didn't answer.

"My name is Robyn," I said.

He gave me a so-what look and bit off another chunk of sandwich. He didn't say anything.

"I've been looking for Trisha Carnegie," I said. "She's in my history class. We were working on a project together and, well, we had this little problem." I smiled again. See how friendly and unthreatening I am, Kenny? "I was wondering if you knew how I could get in touch with her."

Kenny swallowed what was in his mouth, and then wrapped up what remained of his sandwich, which wasn't much, and shoved it into his jacket pocket. Then he got up and started down the bleachers to the athletic field. He didn't look at me and he didn't answer.

"Hey!" I said. I chased after him. "Hey, wait a minute." But he didn't wait for even a second, let alone a minute. He strode back into the school. I scurried after him — no way was I going to let him treat me like I didn't exist. I was going to follow him until he said something — anything — to me.

He disappeared through a door halfway down the hall. I was close behind him, my hand out to push the door open and go after him. But I dropped my hand back to my side when I read the words stencilled on the door: *Boys' Locker Room.* I backed up a few paces and waited. I must have stood there for nearly ten minutes before two thoughts occurred to me: one, if a guy like Kenny Merchant didn't want to talk, he wouldn't, even if it meant he missed all of his classes for the rest of the day, and, two, there was, of course, another door into — and out of — the boys' locker room, the door to the gym. I checked it out. Kenny wasn't there. He was probably long gone.

"So let me get this straight," Morgan said when I caught up with her in the second floor girls' washroom. She was working hard, but without much success, to get a vegetarian chili stain out of her khaki jeans. "You dumped my tray on me so you could go chasing after *Kenny Merchant?*" She rubbed at the stain with a wad of wet soapy paper towel. From what I could see, she was only making it worse.

"I needed to ask him something," I said.

"Since when do you even know Kenny Merchant?" she said. She was scrubbing so hard that the wad of paper towel began to disintegrate. "The guy's so weird. He and Trisha are the king and queen of bizarre. I saw them together one time, sitting on the floor." She stopped scouring the stain and looked thoughtful for a moment. "You think I should have mentioned that to your dad when he asked me about Trisha?"

"You talked to my father?" I said. "How come you didn't tell me?"

"He was here yesterday, asking people about Trisha and who she hung out with. How come *you* didn't tell me that he's looking for her?"

I apologized and filled her in on Trisha and her stepfather.

"So you think I should tell him about Kenny?" Morgan said when I had finished.

"He already knows," I said. "He tried to talk to Kenny."

"Tried to?" She frowned. Then she grinned at me, her eyes sparkling. "That's why you went after Kenny, isn't it? You're working for your dad, aren't you?" she said. "You're spying for him."

"I'm not spying," I said. "And I'm not working for him. I just said I'd ask around, that's all."

"You think Kenny knows where Trisha is?"

"I don't know."

"What did he say?"

"Nothing," I said. "Not one word."

* * *

One thing about going out with — well, *maybe* going out with — a guy who's in open custody is that you always know where he is or, at least, where he's supposed to be. Whenever Nick leaves Somerset, he has to carry a pass that's signed by Somerset's director. He has a pass that gives him permission to go to school. On Mondays, Thursdays, and Fridays, it says he has to be back at Somerset one hour after school is over to do homework and chores and to take part in group sessions. On Wednesday afternoons and evenings he has a job delivering flyer-stuffed community newspapers door to door. He gets a pass that says he has to phone Somerset when he gets to the place where he picks up the newspapers, he has to call again a couple of hours later, and he has to be back at Somerset by curfew, which is eight o'clock every day of the week. He gets another pass on Saturdays so that he can go to his second job, which is walking two, sometimes three, dogs, including a massive beast named Orion. He got hired for that after all the time he spent sort-of volunteering at the animal shelter. And now, because he's been doing so well and because he's going to be released soon, he can usually get a pass for a couple of hours on Sunday — *if* he has all his homework and his chores done. Sometimes he calls me and we get together. And every Tuesday he gets a pass so that he can have supper with his aunt. Nick doesn't have any parents. He's going to live with his aunt after he's released.

This was Tuesday and because I was worried about him, I took the bus over to his aunt's house after school. On the way I thought about how he had acted the last time I saw him. Something was wrong. But was it something with me? Did it have to do with Beej? Or was something else bothering Nick? If so, what?

I stood on the sidewalk for a few minutes after I got off the bus and thought about what I would say. *Hi, Nick. How ya doin', Nick? So, Nick, are we going out or what?*

Right.

If ever there was a question that was guaranteed to send a guy running in the opposite direction, that was it. According to Morgan, guys were commitment-phobes. If you wanted to find out what they were thinking about your relationship, you had to be careful not to scare them, which meant you had to be indirect. So I stopped at a store on my way to his aunt's house and bought the latest issue of *Dogs Today* magazine. Nick loves dogs. He planned to get one after he settled in with his aunt. I decided to tell him that I'd seen the magazine and thought he'd like to read it. I'd see where things went from there.

I was halfway up the sagging porch steps when I heard a crash, followed a split second later by what sounded like something shattering. Then I heard a voice — an angry male voice — say, "Now look what you've done."

I hesitated.

"Pick that up before your aunt gets back," the same male voice said. It was deep and husky, a smoker's voice.

I heard another sharp sound — not a crash, not something breaking, but more like a smack or a slap, followed by a sound that I couldn't identify but that left me with no doubt that something was wrong.

"Hey!" the husky voice said. "Where do you think you're going?"

I stepped back from the door at precisely the moment that it exploded open. Nick almost knocked me over when he burst out onto the porch. He looked at me, but in a funny way, like he didn't really see me.

"Hey!" the voice said again. A shadow filled the doorway. Then the door opened again and a man stepped out. He was big and was wearing a white T-shirt and jeans. He made a grab for Nick, but pulled back when he saw me.

"What do you want?" he said. He kept his eyes hard on me, like he was daring me to blink or look away. I don't know all the reasons why, but right away I didn't like the guy.

"I'm a friend of Nick's," I said.

Nick was shaking his head at me. What? I *wasn't* his friend? No, that wasn't it. He was shaking his head and looking at me as if he didn't want me to say anything at all, maybe didn't even want me to be there.

The man stepped out onto the porch. He was as tall as my father, but a lot bulkier. He looked like he'd make a good bouncer or maybe a champion WWE wrestler. He also looked like he could be a first-class bully — if he wasn't one already, and I had the feeling he was. He gave me a thorough once-over.

"Sorry, sweetheart, but Nick can't come out to play," he said. He made the word 'play' sound like the last thing you'd want your children to be doing. "He's got some business to attend to inside."

I glanced at Nick. He was cradling his left arm in his right hand as he glowered at the big man. Then he turned his back on the man and started down the porch steps. The man reached for him, shoving me aside. He grabbed Nick by the left arm. Nick let out a yowl.

"Inside," the man said. "Now."

"You're hurting him," I said.

The man hung onto Nick, but turned his attention to me.

"Run along, sweetheart," he said, "before—"

That's as far as he got before Nick twisted away from him. Nick grabbed my hand and pulled me down the porch steps two at a time. He pelted down the street, dragging me along with him, running so fast for so long that I thought my lungs would burst. He kept running until we reached a park that ran along the bank of a river that meandered through the city. He pulled me down into the park, away from the streets and the cars and the houses. He didn't stop running until the sounds of traffic had disappeared, and even then all he did was slow down.

"Nick, I need to catch my breath," I said, gasping. I run a couple of times a week, but I'm not a sprinter. I pulled my hand out of his and bent over, breathing hard, my heart pounding. I stumbled over to a bench facing the river and dropped down onto it. "Who was that guy anyway?" I said. "What's going on?"

Nick stood in front of me, his chest heaving from exertion, his face pinched and grey. He was holding his left arm in his right hand again.

"That's Aunt Beverly's boyfriend," he said.

"You never mentioned him before."

"They've been seeing each other for a while," he said grimly. "Now, according to my aunt, it's serious. She says she thinks maybe they have a future."

"Well," I said, "there's that expression — love is

blind." The big man with the husky voice wasn't my idea of boyfriend material, but there was also that other expression — it takes all kinds.

"She says he brings her flowers," Nick said, sounding bitter. "He does stuff around the house for her — apparently he's real handy. He takes her dancing."

"He sounds like every woman's dream," I said, trying to imagine the bullying hulk I had just seen waltzing Nick's aunt across a dance floor. Trying, but not succeeding.

"She's crazy about him." He moved his sore arm tentatively and winced.

"Sit down," I said.

He held his ground.

"Please?" I said.

He stepped a little closer and I took his hand — the good one — and pulled him to the bench. He sat.

"Let me see," I said. I started to push up his left sleeve. I got it high enough to see some deep bruising before he let out a gasp of pain and yanked his arm away.

"Maybe you should get that looked at, Nick."

"It's fine."

"Your face is white."

He didn't say anything. I might as well have been talking to a tree for all the effect I was having.

"What was going on back there?" I said. "I heard a crash."

"I bumped into something."

I waited for more, but in the end had to prompt him.

"When I got to Aunt Bev's, Glen said she was at the hairdresser. He said he was taking her out tonight."

"She's going out with him on a *Tuesday*?" I know Nick's aunt. She's nice and, if you ask me, she really cares about him.

"They're going to celebrate their two-month anniversary," Nick said.

"And your aunt didn't tell you?"

"Glen says she left a message for me at Somerset. But I never got it." He looked angry and hurt.

"It sounded like you and Glen were fighting," I said. "Physically, I mean."

"I fell," he said. But he looked at the ground instead of at me.

"Did he hurt you?" I said.

Nothing.

"That bruise on your arm," I said, "that's at least a couple of days old." There was no way a bruise that colour was the result of what I had just overheard. I remembered Nick slipping on his jacket in the taco place. I wondered if he'd done it to hide the bruise on his arm. "What happened, Nick? How'd you get that bruise?"

He jumped to his feet. "What are you doing here anyway?" he said. "You show up uninvited and you start in with a million questions—"

"I didn't—"

"I don't get along with the guy, okay? I don't like him and he doesn't like me. So what?"

"But if your aunt is serious about him—"

"If she's serious, she's serious. It's none of my business."

"Yeah, but—"

"I gotta go," he said.

"But, Nick—"

He turned and started walking down the footpath that ran along the riverbank. I got up and ran after him. At first when I caught up with him, he pretended I wasn't there and kept walking, looking straight ahead. But after a couple of minutes, he slowed down and took my hand in his. He held it until we reached the bus stop.

"You going back to your aunt's?" I said.

He shook his head. "I think I'll head back to Somerset."

"You sure you don't want to see a doctor about your arm? There's a walk-in clinic over on Franklin." It was a ten-minute bus ride away. "I'll go with you."

He shook his head. "If it still hurts later, I'll get Selma to take a look at it." Selma was one of the onsite counsellors at Somerset. Nick seemed to like her. He let go of my hand and slipped his arm around me instead. "Don't worry about me, okay? I can take care of myself."

It felt good when he held me like that, so close I could feel the warmth of his body. It did not feel good when he released me and climbed up into the bus, especially when I saw the sombre expression on his face.

Chapter Eight

Billy's hand clamped over my arm like a trap snapping shut on a mouse.

"Geeze, Billy—"

"She's coming," he said. He gripped my arm while he watched Morgan enter the cafeteria. She stood just inside the door, scanning faces until she found us. She raised a hand, waved, and started toward us.

"Are you sure I should do this?" Billy said. Sweat had broken out on his forehead.

"Billy, all I said was—"

"Breath mints," he said. "Robyn, do you have any breath mints?"

"Billy, relax, it's only Morgan. Since when do you care what your breath smells like around her?" Besides, it usually smelled just fine — one of the positive by-products of being vegan.

He sprang to his feet, jarring the table so that I had to grab my bottle of juice to keep it from spilling.

"Morgan," he said, as if he were astonished to see

her, as if the three of us didn't have lunch together almost every school day.

"Hey, Billy," she said absently, not so much as glancing at him as she slung her backpack onto the table and started to root around inside it.

When Billy raised his hand to wipe the perspiration from his forehead, I saw a huge stain under his arm. Poor guy, he was really nervous.

"I got my English essay back," Morgan said. She pulled a wad of paper from her backpack and flung it at me. "I can't believe it. Do you have any idea how hard I worked on that? And look what he gave me. Just look."

He was Mr. Turturro, Morgan's English teacher, fresh out of teacher training. A baby, is how Morgan described him. A baby with a (short) past in minor league baseball. The word was that although he had been a good catcher, he was a slow runner, which was why he wasn't still in minor league baseball and had never even come close to making the majors. His nickname when he'd been playing was the Turtle, which of course everybody at school called him now.

"I mean, he's a jock. He teaches phys. ed.," she said. "What genius decided he should teach English, too? What does a *jock* know about literature?"

I picked up the crumpled mess of paper she had tossed at me, smoothed it out with my hand, and looked at the mark printed in red in the upper right-hand corner.

"*B*-plus," I said. "Not bad."

"Not bad?" she said. "I've never gotten a *B*-plus in my life."

It was true. Morgan didn't just have an *A* average. She had a straight-*A record*. She pulled *A*s on every essay, term paper, exam, test, and pop quiz ever thrown at her. She was usually modest about it. Mostly she would read her mark, shrug, give a (sometimes smug) half-smile, and not say anything at all. After all, what was there to say? She always did her best to act as if another *A* was no big deal. The way it looked now, maybe it was true, maybe *A*s *were* no big deal. But *B*s, even *B*-pluses? They were a whole different story.

"It's still the beginning of the year," I said. "Now that you know how Mr. Turturro marks, you'll do better next time."

"*Next* time?" she said. "I did better *this* time. This essay is brilliant."

So much for modesty.

"This is an *A*-plus essay, not a *B*-plus essay," she said. "I can't believe that guy. I mean, he's a *jock*."

That's when Billy decided to chime in. "You know what you need, Morgan? You need to get your mind off school," he said.

I had to give him credit: it was a smooth segue. Too bad his timing was off.

Morgan turned her angry eyes on him. "What I *need*, Billy," she said, "is for the Turtle to give me the mark I deserve. That's what I need."

"Yeah, but he's not going to change—" He shut up when Morgan gave him a look that could have turned molten lava to cold, hard rock in three seconds flat. Flustered, he glanced at me. I think he was looking for encouragement or maybe courage. I looked him in the eyes. I shook my head. I tried to warn him, I really did. But Billy didn't pay attention. He pulled himself up straight and drew in a deep breath. He said, "Morgan, do you want to go out with me this weekend?"

Morgan was looking at me when he said it. She had her mouth open, as if she had been about to speak. It hung open a little longer. Then, slowly, she shifted her eyes from me to Billy.

"What did you say?" If you focused only on the words, you would have thought she was asking for clarification. If you focused on her tone of voice instead, you would have thought she was accusing Billy of some heinous crime.

Billy's face turned pink, then red, then crimson.

"I said . . . I was wondering . . ."

"Did you just ask me out?" Morgan said, incredulous and indignant at the same time.

Billy spluttered and nodded.

"In case you haven't noticed, I'm having the worst day of my life," Morgan said, which reminded me that everything is relative. "And all you can do is make jokes? That *was* a joke, right, Billy?"

"Come on, Morgan," I said.

Morgan is my best friend. So is Billy, but Billy's a boy, so maybe Morgan is more of a best friend. I've known her forever — and I know she's not perfect. Nobody is. I also know that she can get just a little too wrapped up in herself and, when she does, she can be, well, myopic. I'd have been willing to bet that she didn't notice what was glaringly obvious to me — that Billy looked like he had just been slapped. Hard. By her.

Billy's face was still bright red. He stared at me as if I had been responsible for ordering him on what he now realized was a suicide mission. He stood up. I pretended not to notice that Morgan had seen the look he'd given me.

"Billy—" I said. But he stumbled away from the table and ran out of the cafeteria. I turned to Morgan, who was regarding me with unadulterated disapproval.

"You put him up to it," she said. "Don't deny it. It was written all over his face." She snatched her *A*-plus-marked-*B*-plus essay from my hand and jammed it back into her pack.

"Morgan, I just—"

But by then I was talking to her back as she cut between the tables, heading for the door.

Terrific.

As I screwed the lid back onto my bottle of juice, I saw someone watching me from across the room. Kenny Merchant. There was a girl sitting with him. She looked to see where Kenny was looking. When she saw me, she scowled.

I shoved the bottle into my purse, got up, and started weaving my way through the tables toward Kenny. I half expected him to get up and walk away before I got there. Why not? Everyone else was doing it. But he didn't. The girl — her name was Alison something; I'd seen her around, but didn't really know her — said something to him. He barely glanced at her when he answered, but whatever he said sure got a reaction. She straightened out of her slouch as if she'd been jabbed in the back. She said something else, but this time got no answer. She stood up and said something else. Still no answer. She glowered as she pushed by me.

I looked at Kenny.

"Hi," I said. I didn't expect an answer and I didn't get one. "Look, about Trisha . . ."

"You're not a friend of hers," he said. He was telling me, not asking me.

"I never said I was. I said we did a project together and we had a problem—"

"Yeah, well, I don't know anything about her, so you can stop asking me."

"You know she's missing, don't you?" I said. If he knew, he didn't seem to care. Or, if he cared, he didn't show it. It was impossible to read anything on his face. "Her parents are frantic. Her mother is sick."

Nothing.

"Maybe something happened to her," I said. "Don't you care?"

"I already told you, I don't know anything about her."

Right. And one of the main things he didn't know about her was that I wasn't her friend.

"Don't talk to me again," he said. "Don't ask me any more questions. And don't follow me. You got that?"

I looked at him one last time before I turned and walked away. Maybe that teacher my father had spoken to was right. Maybe she had seen Kenny and Trisha together. But I couldn't imagine their conversations going any better than mine just had. Kenny Merchant wasn't exactly Mr. Congeniality.

As I was making my way out of the cafeteria, I got that prickly back-of-the-neck feeling that makes you think that someone is staring at you. I turned, but all I saw were kids — kids leaving the cafeteria, kids entering the cafeteria, kids just hanging around outside the cafeteria — none of whom were paying any attention to me. Most of them were in pairs or trios or larger groups — except for one person who was standing by herself. Alison, the girl who had been with Kenny. She was rummaging in her purse for something. I started to turn away. Then, maybe because there was something about the way she was fumbling around, I took a second look. This time our eyes met because this time she was staring right back at me. She kept staring at me, too, giving me a condescending, challenging look, as if she were daring me to do something, but I couldn't figure out what or even why I would. I turned to walk away.

"Hey," a voice said. Someone jolted my shoulder from behind. I spun around, angry. It was Alison, with the same scowl and the same winning personality, except that now she seemed to be sizing me up. "You stay away from him, okay?"

"What?" What was she talking about? "You mean Kenny?"

"You're not his type," she said. "You don't have a chance with him. You know where he lived last?" She paused dramatically before telling me. "Somerset." Well, what do you know; one of the rumours circulating about Kenny Merchant was true. "You know what Somerset is?"

"Yes, I do," I said. She took a closer look at me, surprised, I think, by my answer. Then I caught the look in her eyes. She really thought I was interested in him. She was jealous. People are only jealous when they feel insecure. Maybe she liked Kenny, but obviously she wasn't confident he felt the same way about her. So here she was trying to stake out her territory, trying to warn me away from him. She wouldn't be doing that unless she felt threatened by me. I wondered if she felt threatened by Trisha, too.

"What about Trisha Carnegie?" I said.

"What about her?"

"You think *she* has a chance with Kenny?"

Her expression became more sullen and resentful.

"I don't know why he wastes his time with her," she said.

"So he *is* interested in her?"

That earned me a sharp look. "No," she said. Then her face softened and she said, "At least, not the way you think." She didn't seem sure, though. "He's interested in *me*. We're going out." She studied me again. "You sure you're not after him?"

"Not even remotely," I said. Then, because she could have read that a couple of ways, not all of them favourable, I said, "Although I'm sure he's very nice."

I caught the hint of a smile before she said, "He has his good qualities."

"Look, Alison, I'm not interested in Kenny. I'm interested in Trisha. You heard the announcement in homeroom last Friday, didn't you? She's missing. Her mother is worried."

Alison snorted derisively. What did that *mean?*

"Yeah, I heard the announcement," Alison said. "But I don't know where she is, and I don't care. I think she's a freak. She talks to herself, you know? I've seen her in the hall, muttering under her breath like one of those bag ladies you see downtown. It's like the rest of the world doesn't exist for her. When she ran out of here one morning last week, she slammed right into me. She almost knocked me over. And you know what? She didn't stop, didn't apologize. Nothing. If she's gone, good riddance."

"What do you mean, she ran out of here?"

"What I said. I saw her rooting around in her locker, then, boom, she ran down the hall and slammed right into me."

"When was this?"

"What difference does it make?"

"Was it Wednesday? Wednesday morning?"

She looked surprised. "Yeah," she said. "Just after the late bell rang."

Just after I'd yelled at her. Just after I had told her that I didn't care about her mother being sick, that no one did. "You saw her leave school?"

"I just said I did, didn't I?"

"Did you see her after that?"

"No," she said, sounding impatient now. "Why?"

"Her mother is sick. Really sick," I said. "And it's not helping that she's worried about Trisha. I promised to help find her." Which was true. I had promised my father. If Alison got the impression that I had promised Trisha's mother, well, that was her problem. "I heard someone say they'd seen Trisha and Kenny together. I thought he might know something."

She shrugged.

"But he knows her, right?"

Finally she said, "Kenny doesn't talk about other people. He respects their privacy, you know?" Boy, he sounded just like Nick. "But I get the feeling he knows Trisha from before."

Before? "Before what? Before he transferred to this school, you mean?"

She nodded. "I've heard people talk about her. I heard she's a runaway queen. Something bad happens at home and, boom, she hits the streets. I think maybe that's where Kenny met her. He's spent some time on the street, too." Another rumour about Kenny turned out to be true. "I get the feeling he identifies with her."

Based on my two brief encounters with Kenny, I found it hard to believe that he could identify with anyone. He came across as hostile and indifferent.

"Why would he identify with Trisha? What do they have in common?"

"They both have messed-up parents," Alison said. "It's what makes them run. Well, it's what used to make Kenny run. His dad is a real creep. Drinks too much and gets really mean when he does. He was always telling Kenny he's stupid and worthless, stuff like that. Really building Kenny's self-esteem, you know? His mother isn't much better. By the time Kenny was twelve, he'd run away something like ten times. After that, he fixed it so they'd never send him back home again."

"Meaning?"

She gave me another look. "I *told* you. He was in Somerset. He's living in another group home now, you know, for kids who can't live at home for whatever reason. He's settling down a little. He's coming to school. Well, most days he is."

That explained a lot about Kenny. Still, I wondered . . . "Trisha's parents aren't like Kenny's. She runs away when she gets mad at her mother, not because her parents treat her badly. Her stepfather seems like a nice guy."

"Yeah, *seems*." Alison shook her head. "You never know what someone is really like until you live with them. I caught Kenny and Trisha together one time. She was whining about her stepfather. I missed the specifics, but, boy, is she ever pissed off at her mother for marrying the guy. She wouldn't feel that way if he was such a nice guy, would she? I bet you anything that's why she took off."

Or maybe, this time, it was someone else she didn't like. For instance, me.

"Do you think Kenny knows where she is?"

"If he does, he won't tell."

"Not even if *you* asked him?"

"No way," Alison said. "*If* Kenny knows where

she is and *if* he wanted me to know, he'd tell me. If not . . ." She shrugged. "I told you. Kenny likes his privacy, so he respects other people's privacy."

I thought about Nick, who had seemed a lot like Kenny when I'd first met him and who probably still seemed that way to a lot of people. I wondered if maybe Kenny showed Alison a side of himself that he hid from the rest of the world. It wouldn't have surprised me.

"Maybe you could tell Kenny that Trisha's mother is really worried," I said. "You know, in case he happens to see her."

"It's none of my business," she said. She studied me for another few moments before finally shaking her head and walking away.

* * *

When I left school that afternoon, I was surprised to find Nick waiting for me at my bus stop. I wasn't surprised to see his left arm in a sling.

"Is it broken?" I said.

"Sprained."

"Are you going to be able to do your job?" On Wednesdays after school Nick reported to a drop-off point to collect bundles of newspapers that he loaded onto a little cart. He pulled the cart with one hand and threw the rolled-up papers onto people's porches with the other.

"I'll manage," he said.

Not that I didn't want to see him, but, "Shouldn't you be on your way there now?"

"I have a little time," he said. "Come on."

He led me to a hole-in-the-wall restaurant across the street from my school. At lunch time and most days after school, the place was usually crammed with kids. Today, for some reason, it was quiet. We bought some Cokes at the counter and carried them to a booth at the back — Nick sure did love back booths. I slid onto one of the benches. Nick sat opposite me. He said, "I'm sorry for the way I acted, okay?"

Maybe he expected me to say, okay, sure, no problem. Some people are like that. They act like jerks and then when they get around to apologizing, they expect that to be the end of it. Their attitude is: *I apologized — what more do you want?* I took a sip of my Coke.

Nick leaned forward across the table, paying real attention to me for the first time in awhile. "Hey, Robyn? I said I'm sorry. So everything is okay now, right?"

"It's a nice change to have someone apologize to me instead of telling me to mind my own business or walking out on me," I said. "Which, in case you're interested, is the kind of week I've been having."

"I really am sorry," he said, and, boy, when those purple eyes of his fixed on mine, I believed him. "I get so mad sometimes," he said. It wasn't the first time he'd admitted it to me — he had anger management issues. "But I'm trying. I really am." He reached out and laid one of his hands — his right hand — over one of mine.

"I know. I'm just having a bad day," I said. "Morgan yelled at me. Billy is treating me like I'm Judas. And this guy, Kenny Merchant, told me to get lost and stay lost." And there it was, just for a second: a flash of surprise in his eyes, like summer lightning — you think you see it, but before you can be sure, it's gone. "You know him, Nick?"

"Who?" Acting like he hadn't caught the name. I might have believed it, too, except for that flash.

"Kenny Merchant," I said. "You know him?"

"Why?"

Why? "Because I think maybe he knows something about a girl who's missing." I told him about Trisha. When I said her name, he looked down at the table. "So, do you know him?"

He shrugged, but it came off lopsided because his right shoulder did all the work. "No," he said.

"Oh," I said. "Because he was at Somerset, too."

Anyone watching us would have thought he was looking directly at me. But he wasn't. Not anymore. Now his eyes were focused a little to the left of me, avoiding my eyes.

"Must have been before my time," he said.

"Are you sure?" I said. He tensed up, angry, I think, that I doubted him. "Trisha's father is a friend of my dad's."

Nick liked my father. I think he admired him. But all he said was, "Sorry, I don't know Kenny what's-his-name." Then he said, "I have to get to work."

He lifted his glass — with his right hand — and drained it. Then he stood up and dug some money from his back pocket — again with his right hand.

"What did you tell them?" I said as he threw some coins on the table.

"About what?"

"What do you think, Nick? About your arm."

"Robyn, I can't be late. I'll get into trouble."

I got up and followed him out of the restaurant. "Did you tell them what he did?" I said.

"Tell who?"

"At Somerset." I was struggling to keep my temper now. "Did you tell them what Glen did? You could report him, Nick. If he assaulted you, you could press charges."

"Robyn, leave me alone about that, okay?" He sounded annoyed.

"They must have asked you about it."

"I already told you. I fell," he said. "It's no big deal."

"Nick, I heard him at your aunt's house. I met him, remember?"

His bus lumbered toward us. Nick stepped in close to me and kissed me lightly. His lips were soft and sweet, and I wrapped my arms around him, gently, so I wouldn't hurt him. "I'll call you later," he said. "If I can, okay?"

I said okay. I watched him climb up into the bus, his right hand cradling his left elbow in the sling until the last minute, when he had to show his bus pass. I watched him turn and walk down the aisle where he found a seat near the window. He looked at me as the bus pulled away. Looked and even smiled, and I thought, he thinks I believed him. He thinks I don't know he's lying. But I did. About Kenny, about Glen, about falling. I knew it for a fact.

Chapter Nine

When I got home, I found my mother curled up on the couch in her bathrobe, her hair wrapped in a towel. She had the TV on, which was startling enough. My mother doesn't watch much TV. She especially doesn't watch sitcom re-runs. But that was exactly what she was doing when I walked in. She was also eating ice cream right from the container, which is something else she never does. Or, at least, something she hasn't done since right after she and my father split up. She told me at the time that separating from my father was the right thing to do, but she cried a lot when she thought I couldn't hear her (mostly late at night), and she'd scooped her way through enough ice cream to keep a small town in cool treats for an entire summer. It had taken a couple of months of serious gym work for her to lose all the inches it had added to her butt and thighs.

"Are you and Ted still taking a break?" I said.

"I really don't want to talk about it, Robyn." She shovelled another spoonful of ice cream into her mouth.

The thing was, I wanted to talk about it. "Did Ted break up with you, Mom? Is that why you're acting like this?" I couldn't think of anything else that could make her this miserable.

She reached for the remote and turned off the TV. Then she snapped the lid back on the ice cream container, got up, and went into the kitchen. I followed her.

"Is that what happened, Mom? Did he dump you?"

She put the ice cream back into the freezer before turning to face me.

"I said I don't want to talk about it, Robyn, and I mean it." She sounded impatient and annoyed that someone — me — had interrupted her ice cream and TV extravaganza. She sounded like that more and more often lately. I didn't like it, and I didn't see why I should have to put up with it.

"I'm going to Dad's," I said.

"No, you're not."

"I can go to Dad's whenever I want."

"You were at your father's all weekend and a couple of days after school this week so far. You should spend more time here with me."

"Why? So I can watch you mope around and whenever I ask you what's going on, you can tell me you don't want to talk about it?"

She relented a little. "I'm sorry," she said. "Look, why don't I get dressed and we'll go out to dinner, just the two of us? We haven't done that in a while. What do you say?"

I said okay. I said it because I thought it would make her happy, not because I thought there was a chance she would tell me what was going on. Good thing, too.

Nick called my cell phone while I was out with my mother, but I'd left it at home. I didn't want anything to interrupt our time together, even though it turned out that any interruption (gale-force hurricane, house-sucking tornado . . .) would have been welcome. My mother was not in the mood to talk — about anything.

Nick had left a message: he had to make a stop downtown after school tomorrow, on his way back to Somerset. He told me where he was going to be and asked if I could meet him. He said if I couldn't make it, it was no big deal. I wasn't sure how I felt about that.

* * *

The next morning, I had a dentist appointment, which meant that I didn't have to go to school first thing. By the time my teeth were gleaming, it was almost noon, so instead of going directly back to school, I stopped by my father's place. I was pretty sure Mr. Jarvis had said something to him about Nick. I wanted to ask him what it was. I wanted to do it in person so that I could see his face if he started to get evasive.

When he didn't answer the buzzer, I let myself in. He wasn't there, so I made myself some lunch. He still hadn't appeared by the time I had finished eating, so I went back downstairs. As I stepped out onto the sidewalk, a man got out of a car parked at the curb. It was Carl Hanover. He forced a smile onto his lips, but there were dark lines under his eyes and he sounded tired when he greeted me. I pictured him sitting beside the telephone with his sick wife, both of them waiting for it to ring, *willing* it to ring.

"Hi, Robyn," he said. "I talked to your father the other day. He told me you were going to ask around at school to see if anyone had heard anything from Trisha or had any idea where she might be. I can't tell you how much Denise and I appreciate that."

I said that I hadn't been able to find out anything. I didn't tell him about Kenny because I'd already struck out twice and I didn't want to get his hopes up.

"Still, we appreciate your help, Robyn," he said. He pulled an envelope from his pocket. "I was just going to drop these off for your father. I gave him a picture of Trisha, but it wasn't a very good one. She never gets her picture taken at school. These are some snapshots her mother took. I thought they could be useful."

"He isn't home," I said. "But if you want, I can give them to him later."

A genuine smile appeared on his sad, tired face. "Would you?" He handed the envelope to me. "Her mother can hardly sleep. She keeps hoping that Trisha will call, but so far nothing." He shook his head. "I bet you never give your parents anything to worry about, do you, Robyn?"

I said I wasn't so sure about that.

I looked for Morgan and Billy when I got to sch. had called Morgan a couple of times the night before, but she hadn't called me back. I wondered if she was still mad at me. I had called Billy, too, with the same result. I felt even worse about him. I was used to Morgan doing her drama queen thing — a lot of things made her angry. But I was not used to Billy looking so crushed and humiliated. I wanted to reassure myself that he was okay.

I couldn't find either of them.

I was thinking about Morgan and Billy while I stood on the corner where Nick had said he'd meet me. I had arrived a few minutes early and was scanning the crowded streets for a tall, good-looking guy with his arm in a sling. Instead I spotted Kenny Merchant sauntering down the street toward me. After talking to Alison, I was sure that if anyone had an idea where Trisha was, it would be Kenny. He was close enough to touch now, but he still didn't notice me — until I stepped out in front of him.

"Hey," he said, annoyed at finding an obstacle in his path. Then he recognized me. He shook his head and started to circle around me.

"I need to talk to Trisha and I think you know where she is," I said.

He kept walking, as if he hadn't heard me. Boy, was I ever getting tired of his tough-guy attitude. I grabbed him by the arm.

"Come on, Kenny, you have to tell me where she is. It's important. If you don't—"

"If I don't, you'll do what?" he said. He wasn't much taller than me, but he looked like the kind of guy who didn't mind getting physical, who maybe even enjoyed it. "You'll call the cops? Be my guest. I'll tell them the same thing I already told you — I don't know where she is. And you know what? They won't care. They're not even looking for her. She hasn't done anything wrong."

I'd been going to say, if you don't, her mother will be devastated. I'd been going to tell him how sick Trisha's mother was, in case he didn't know. I'd been going to appeal to his compassion. I'd even been willing to assume, based on what Alison had told me, that he was capable of compassion. Now I wasn't so sure.

I looked him in the eye now. "You know that for a fact, right, Kenny?" I said. "You know all that about somebody you say you don't know anything about."

He looked at me, his eyes sharp and cold. It reminded me of the way Nick used to look when he was angry. Then Kenny did something that Nick would never have done. He grabbed me, hard, and yanked me toward him, so close that I could feel his breath hot on my face and see the black flecks in his mud-coloured eyes.

"Stay away from me," he said. "You got that?"

He shoved me away so hard that I lost my balance. My hands flew out, feeling for something to grab onto. But there was nothing. As I pitched backward, I made myself curl a little so that when I hit the cement, it would be my butt and maybe my back that made contact, not my head.

But I never hit the cement. Instead, someone grabbed me around the waist and suddenly I wasn't falling anymore. Then whoever had caught me put me back on my feet and said, "What do you think you're doing?" It was Nick. His question was directed at Kenny, not at me.

"What's it to you?" Kenny said.

Nick kept his arm around me, but I felt it tense up. He must have looked pretty fierce because Kenny backed up, but only half a pace.

"She was bothering me, okay?" he said. "Not that it's any of your business, D'Angelo, but she's a real pain."

Well, well. Nick had told me he didn't know Kenny. But Kenny sure seemed to know Nick.

"When you push my girlfriend around, it's my business," Nick said.

Girlfriend! I pulled away a little so that I could look at Nick. He was still holding me tightly around the waist. Even with his left arm in a sling, he looked fierce. He was taller than Kenny and had a little more weight to him. He was staring at Kenny as if he were daring him to try something — anything.

"I'm okay," I murmured to Nick.

"See?" Kenny said, stepping forward, cocky again. "She's fine. So there's no problem."

"If you ever touch her again, there'll be a big problem," Nick said. His eyes locked onto Kenny's for a few seconds. Kenny was the first to look away.

He glowered at me, maybe trying to scare me since it was obvious he didn't scare Nick. "You hear me?" Nick said.

"Yeah. I hear you."

They stared at each other a little longer before Kenny blinked, then turned and walked away. Nick watched him go before relaxing his grip on me and looking me over.

"You hurt?" he said.

I shook my head. I was thinking about what he had said. Girlfriend. He had described me as his girlfriend.

"Come on." He slipped his good arm around my waist again and led me to a coffee shop. We went inside, ordered hot chocolate for me, regular coffee for him — and sat near the window. I couldn't stop thinking about what he had said, about that one glorious word that I wanted to hear him say again. He might have too, if I had been willing to let things be. Instead I said, "I thought you didn't know Kenny Merchant."

Nick didn't look guilty or embarrassed at being caught in a lie. He didn't avert his eyes this time, either. Instead, he looked directly at me and said, "I owe him. When you owe a guy and someone starts asking about him, you don't talk about him, you don't talk about his business."

"What is that?" I said. "Some kind of guy code?"

He shook his head and sighed, as if I just didn't get it, as if we lived in completely different worlds, which, I guess, we did.

"There were a couple of guys at the place I was in before Somerset," he said. "Tough guys, you know? Real bullies. When I first got there, they gave me a hard time. A *really* hard time, you know what I mean, Robyn?"

Based on his intensity, I had a pretty good idea.

"What about the staff?" I said.

Nick laughed, but there was nothing jolly about the sound.

"The staff were okay," he said. "But they can't be everywhere all the time. They can't be in all the rooms all night. They can't be in the bathroom all the time. They can't be in the laundry room all the time. You know?"

I was getting the picture.

"Kenny helped me out," Nick said. "He knows Joey, through his cousin." Joey was Nick's step-brother. He was doing time on a charge of criminal negligence causing death. "Kenny didn't have to help me, but he did. And when a guy puts himself out for you like that, you owe him."

"I think he might know where Trisha is," I said.

Nick shook his head. "You can't keep messing around in other people's lives," he said.

Keep messing around? "Excuse me?" I said.

"Everybody doesn't need you to get involved in their business," he said. "Me, okay, that was one thing and I guess I appreciate that." I'd helped him out of trouble — *serious* trouble — a couple of months back.

"You *guess?* And what do you mean, *everybody?*

You make it sound as if all I do is meddle." If you ask me, I had done as much for him as Kenny had — maybe more. But it was obvious that he didn't feel he owed me the way he owed Kenny.

He reached for my hand. I yanked it off the table and deposited it in my lap. Nick shook his head again.

"You kept me from doing something stupid and I'm grateful. I really am," he said. "But you have this tendency to want to get involved in things that are none of your business, like with this girl who's missing or the thing with Glen—"

"Glen who twisted your arm or hit you or did whatever it took to put your arm in a sling? Glen who probably put that bruise on your arm, too? Is that the *thing* you mean?"

He stared at me for a moment. "I can never tell whether you sound more like your mother or your father. I think maybe it's a combination of both."

"A girl is missing," I said.

Not a flicker.

I reached in my bag for the envelope Mr. Hanover had given me, opened it, pulled out a picture of Trisha, and slapped it down on the table in front of him. "Here," I said. "She's the girl I'm talking about, just so we're one hundred percent clear. She's a real girl with real parents who are worried sick about her."

Nick looked down at the picture. "You mean *parent*," he said without looking up. "Singular. Her mother. The guy, he's not her real dad, right?"

"So what?" I said. "You think only *real* fathers

care?" Knowing Nick, based on his own experience, that was probably exactly what he thought. Then, wait a minute. "How do you know that? Or maybe you *don't* know Trisha Carnegie the same way you didn't know Kenny Merchant."

Up came those purple eyes of his, away from the picture and back to me.

"Your dad's a great guy," he said. "And I don't just mean because he's successful and funny and fair, you know, the way he looks at people. I mean because of how he cares about you. He really loves you. And your mom? She's smart and she can be pretty tough, but she loves you, too. I don't think there's anything she wouldn't do for you. You know what that makes you?"

"What? You're trying to tell me I'm spoiled?"

"I'm trying to tell you you're lucky. You're lucky that you have two parents who care more about what happens to you than they do about what happens to themselves. A lot of kids I know, kids at Somerset, for sure the kids at the drop-in centre, they're not nearly so lucky. A lot of them left home because one or both of their parents can't stand them, don't care what happens to them, or just plain don't want them around. Some of them don't even have parents. Some of them have been bounced from foster home to foster home their whole lives. Nobody in the world cares what happens to them." He reached for my hand again, and again I refused to let him have it. "Robyn, did you ever stop to think that maybe this girl you're looking for had a good reason to leave home?"

"Do you know where she is?"

He looked me straight in the eye and said, flat out and with not even a millisecond's hesitation, "No." Then he said, "But to tell you the truth, if I did know, I don't think I'd tell you or anyone else, at least not unless she told me I could."

"Thanks a *lot*."

"Have you ever run away, Robyn?"

"Of course not."

"Well, I have. Plenty of times. I usually ran when I was too afraid to be at home, you know, on account of the guy my mother was living with." Nick's stepfather. The guy who liked to beat up on people. The guy who had given Nick the scar that sliced diagonally across the right side of his face. The guy who had made him an orphan. "I ran away and stayed gone as long as I could. And, Robyn? If anyone I knew had ever told my stepfather where I was . . ." He shook his head. "You don't know what really goes on at Trisha's house, just like you don't know what really goes on at my aunt's house."

Whoa, wait a minute! What did *that* mean?

"But you have to respect people and their privacy," he said. "You have to respect their reasons for doing what they do."

"What about her mother? She's really sick."

"*Her* mother," he said, "not yours. That makes it *her* decision."

"Come on, Nick. You *know* Kenny. And I'm pretty sure Kenny knows something. You could help me find out."

114

He shook his head.

"There's another reason I need to find her, Nick. A personal reason."

That's when I saw Beej. She entered the restaurant just as Nick turned his head to look out the window. She adjusted her ratty backpack on her shoulder and started toward our table, her eyes jumping from me to Nick and back to me again. As she reached out to touch Nick on the shoulder to get his attention, her eyes went to the photograph of Trisha that was lying on the table between us, and her hand froze in mid-air. She stared at the photo, her mouth hanging open a little in surprise. She kept staring at it. She knows her, I thought. Beej knows Trisha Carnegie. But how?

I remembered the first time I'd met Beej. She had been sitting outside the drop-in centre and someone had whistled. When I'd looked around, I'd seen someone I recognized — Kenny — on the other side of the street. He'd stood there for a moment, munching on a hot dog, and then he'd walked away. At the time, I hadn't made a connection. It hadn't even occurred to me that he might have been the person who had whistled. But right after Kenny had moved on, Beej had said that she had to go. What if she'd gone to meet someone?

Trisha knew Kenny.

Kenny had spent some time on the street.

Beej spent a lot of time on the street.

Did Beej know Kenny, too?

That day I'd met her, had she been dashing off to meet Kenny? Had his whistle been a signal to her?

Beej looked from the pictures of Trisha to Nick, who had just become aware that someone was standing behind him, but hadn't yet seen who it was. He started to turn in his chair, but by then Beej was staring at Nick and shaking her head slowly, as if she didn't want to believe whatever it was that she was thinking. The look she gave me made it clear that she held me responsible. She started to back away as Nick slid out of his chair.

"Beej?" he said. He looked confused when she continued to back away. He followed her gaze to the pictures on the table and his eyes went wide. "Hey, Beej—"

She turned and ran out of the restaurant. Nick got up and raced after her. They had both vanished by the time I got outside. I stood there and waited for ten, fifteen, twenty minutes, sure that Nick would come back. He didn't.

* * *

I was sitting in the living room area of my father's loft when he got home. He looked mildly surprised to see me.

"Did you have a fight with your mother?" he said.

"No. Why?"

"I know that face, Robbie. Something's wrong."

I gave him the envelope of photographs that Carl Hanover had left with me. Delivering them was one of the reasons I had come to my father's place.

He glanced at the photos and said, "You sure everything is okay between you and your mother?"

"Dad, I already told you. We didn't have a fight."

"So she's okay then, right? Because it sure looked like something was bothering her the other night."

"She's fine," I said, and then I couldn't help it, I looked away from him, just for a split second. He caught it — he always caught it — and he knew what it meant, that I wasn't being completely honest. But he didn't say anything, I think because he understood that my mother was fanatical about her privacy and that I had promised to respect it.

"So if it's not about your mother," he said, "what *is* bothering you, Robbie?" He looked genuinely concerned and genuinely interested. When I still didn't say anything, he didn't push me. Instead, he said, "It's getting late. Are you hungry? I'm going to start supper."

He went into the kitchen. I trailed after him and watched him stare into the fridge. "How about an omelette?" he said. "Salad on the side? Toast, lightly browned, just the way you like it?" He pulled out eggs, mushrooms, and cheese.

"It's Nick," I said finally.

"Oh." He didn't sound surprised.

"You've heard something about him, haven't you, Dad? I can tell by the way you act every time I mention him."

My father set everything down onto the counter and turned to look at me. He seemed so serious all of a sudden that it scared me. "I don't know much, Robbie," he said. "I just heard it hasn't been smooth sailing for him lately."

"What do you mean? What did you hear?"

"You know I like Nick, don't you, Robbie? He's done some pretty stupid things, but I think that, basically, he's a decent kid. You know that, right?"

I said I did, but I was getting a queasy feeling in my stomach.

"And I know you like him. Maybe a lot. But you also know enough about his background, and about his" — he hesitated — "his *problems* to know that sometimes Nick makes things harder on himself that they need to be."

I couldn't stand it anymore. "What did you hear, Dad? Does it have anything to do with a guy named Glen?"

Now my father looked surprised. "Nick told you about him?"

"I met him," I said. "I told Nick if I were him, I'd call the cops on Glen."

A strange expression appeared on my father's face. "Robbie," he said, "Glen *is* the cops. That's how I heard."

Wait a second. "I met him, Dad. Well, sort of. That guy's a *cop?*"

"Patrol officer," my father said. "A good one, too."

"What did he tell you?"

"That things aren't going so well between Nick and his aunt. And that Nick may not be able to live with her when he finishes at Somerset. He may have to live in a group home. Nick hasn't had a lot of stability in his life in the past few years, Robbie. Maybe he doesn't know how to handle it."

"According to *Glen*," I said.

"Robbie—"

"Did he tell you he hurt Nick?"

My father frowned. "Hurt him? How?"

"They got into some kind of fight. Nick's arm is badly sprained." I caught a look on my father's face. "What?"

"Nick and Glen got into a fight?" he said. I nodded. "Who started it?"

"I don't know—"

"For all you know, it could have been Nick."

"Dad!" I couldn't believe he was saying that. I couldn't believe he was blaming Nick.

"All I'm saying, Robbie, is that there are two sides to every story and we don't know what those two sides are. But I do know that Glen Ross is a well-respected police officer and that Nick is a kid who has trouble keeping a grip on his temper. Robbie." His voice became softer now. "When I said I like Nick, I meant it. I think he's got a lot of potential."

"Potential?"

"But I also think you should be careful."

"*Careful?* Of what? You think Nick would ever hurt me?"

"Physically?" My father looked surprised. "No. But I think he could break your heart."

Why was he telling me that? Did he feel the same way as my mother did? Did he wish I'd go out with someone more . . . normal? And why was he so quick to believe that Nick was the problem instead of this cop?

"I'm not telling you not to see Nick," my father

said. "I'm not saying he *will* hurt you. And I'm not lying when I say I like him. If I could think of some way to help him, I'd do it. I'm just saying that I think you should be careful. You're my daughter. I love you. I don't want to see you hurt. Okay?"

I said okay even though I didn't feel okay about it. I let him cajole me into helping him make supper: I sliced the mushrooms and grated the cheese. While he cooked the omelette, I made the salad. But the whole time, I was thinking about Nick — about what kind of problems he was having with his aunt, about whether he could solve those problems before his time was up at Somerset, and about how much those problems had to do with Glen. I was worried about him. He'd been trying so hard to turn things around, and he really deserved to have something good happen to him. I wanted him to be happy for a change.

I put my thoughts aside when my father and I sat down to eat. I felt I'd heard enough of my father's feelings on the subject of Nick. So instead I asked him about Carmine Doig.

"Did you find out anything?" I said.

"You mean, was it really an accident?" He shrugged and took a bite of toast. "The police are going by the fire marshal's report, which says it was accidental. So as far as the police are concerned, it's case closed. I can't press the fire marshal for any details because he's dead. I've been trying to get the insurance company to take another look at it. They paid out a lot of money. But they won't even talk to me. They're stonewalling me."

I was surprised to hear that. "Mom always says you could get a confession out of a priest," I said.

"I could if he didn't have a grudge against me," my father said. "I've had some dealings with the guy who's in charge. Let's just say that the only thing he'd be willing to do for me is send flowers to my funeral."

"It sounds to me like you're not satisfied with either the fire marshal's report or the way the insurance company handled the claim," I said.

"Something's not right about the way it happened," my father said.

"What do you mean?"

"A lot of owners board their horses at Doig's stables. Five horses died in the fire. Fifteen were rescued." He took another bite of toast. "Fourteen of the fifteen that were rescued belonged to other owners. Four of the five that died belonged to Carmine Doig."

"So?"

"So, there's stable hand who lives in a cabin at the end of the property. He said he was asleep when the fire started. He said by the time he reached the stable, the fire was blazing and there was smoke everywhere."

"With all those horses, didn't they have a sprinkler system or something?"

"They did," my father said. "But it was undergoing routine maintenance. In fact, the fire marshal's report says that the fire started because of a short in some of the equipment that the repair guys had left in the stables."

"What about the fire alarm?"

"The alarm went off. Besides the stables and the stable hand's cabin, there's a house on the property — a sort of country manor, really. The Doig family uses it sometimes. Sometimes the horses' owners stay there, too. There's a permanent housekeeper. He was there that night. He's the one who called the fire department. But the place is way out in the country. The closest fire department is twenty kilometres away and it's volunteer-run. They know what they're doing, but it takes time. While they were waiting for the fire truck to show up, the stable hand said he started to get the horses out."

"Don't you believe him?"

"I asked him why he didn't start by evacuating Doig's horses. After all, Doig is his employer. He said they were kept at the far end of the stable and that he assumed the trainer was taking care of them."

I repeated my question.

"I asked him if he actually saw the trainer. He said it was dark and confusing. There were skittish horses everywhere. And a lot of smoke. And people who weren't doing much good — a horse owner and his wife who were visiting from Florida, and the manager of one of Doig's construction companies. They had no idea how to handle panicky horses. The stable hand said all he could think about was getting as many animals out as possible, and that's what he did."

I waited. I had no idea what he was thinking or why he was suspicious.

"The police talked to the guy. So did the fire marshal. So did the insurance adjuster—"

"Insurance adjuster?"

"The person who has final say on an insurance claim, who decides whether the insurance company will pay the claim and how much they'll pay."

"And? Did the stable hand tell different stories to different people?"

"I know what he said to the police and to the fire marshal — I've seen the reports. I'm not so sure what he said to the insurance adjuster, but I don't see why it would be any different."

I didn't get it. "So that's good, right?"

"It is if it's the truth." He took a bite of omelette.

Well, that answered my question. My father obviously had some doubts.

"What part don't you believe?" I said.

"I'm not sure," he said. "To be honest, I'm not even sure he's lying. It's not so much *what* he said that bothers me. It's *how* he told it. He seemed awfully nervous for a guy who was telling the same story for the fifth, maybe the tenth, time."

The buzzer for the downstairs door sounded. My father got up to answer it. This time I recognized the voice when I heard it. It was Carl Hanover. My father gave me a look that told me he was sorry for the interruption. Then he pushed the button and told Mr. Hanover to come up.

I don't think it would be possible for a person to look more upset than Mr. Hanover did when he came through the door.

"I'm sorry, Mac," he said. "I should have called first. But I was in the neighbourhood and, well, I just can't seem to concentrate on anything."

My father told him not to worry. He asked him if he'd like something to eat. Mr. Hanover said no. Then my father said, "How about a cup of coffee?" and Mr. Hanover said yes, thank you, to that. He sat at the table while my father went to get him a cup. He looked at me with red, watery eyes that made me think the poor guy hadn't slept in days. Maybe Trisha resented her mother for marrying him, and maybe Kenny sympathized with her (although it was hard to imagine Kenny sympathizing with anyone), but his concern looked genuine to me. I felt sorry for him.

My father put a cup of coffee in front of him and said, "I wish I could tell you I've made progress, Carl, but the truth is, I haven't. I've done the usual — checked with her bank to see if Trisha has used her bank card. She hasn't. I went around to all the places you said she frequents — the mall, the library, the park down by the lake. No one remembers seeing anyone who fits her description. I've also talked to people who are on the street a lot — taxi drivers, newspaper delivery truck drivers, bus drivers. Nobody's seen her. So either she's not in the downtown area, or she's really lying low."

The longer my father talked, the more Mr. Hanover shrank in his chair. He wrapped both hands around the mug of steaming coffee. I thought about how my father might look if I were to vanish. I decided he'd look a lot like Mr. Hanover. I also thought about what it must be like to *be* Mr. Hanover, to have a weird stepdaughter who had never accepted him and a wife who was sick, and to know that it was physically hurting his wife that her daughter had run away. I thought how worried he must be about *her*, too.

"Robyn has been asking around school, but she's drawn a blank, too, haven't you, Robbie?" my father said.

I hadn't told my father yet about Kenny Merchant. Nor had I told him about Beej's reaction when she had seen Trisha's picture. I told myself that it was because there was really nothing to tell — but that wasn't quite true. Mostly I'd been thinking about what Nick had said to me — you have to respect people's reasons for doing what they do; it was Trisha's business, not mine; it was up to Trisha to decide if and when she went home. I also thought about what Nick had said about me and my parents, and about how my home life was so different from his own, from Kenny's, from Beej's. And, maybe, from Trisha's.

I thought, too, about Nick catching me and holding me and telling Kenny, *You push around my girlfriend, it's my business. If you ever touch her again, there'll be a big problem.* Nick holding me, Nick warning (threatening?) Kenny. Then I thought about Nick telling me that even if he knew where Trisha was, he probably wouldn't tell me. In other words, when it came to something important, something he thought of as a matter of principle, Nick didn't completely trust me. Not yet. Maybe never, if I said anything to my father or Mr. Hanover about what I suspected.

I thought about my father saying, *Who started it? For all you know, it could have been Nick,* and believing,

I think, that it had probably been Nick because otherwise he would have to believe it had been Glen, the good cop. And of course a cop — well, an ex-cop — was always ready to take the word of another cop or, at least, to give him the benefit of the doubt.

"Robbie?" my father said. "I said you didn't come up with anything at school. Isn't that right?"

"That's right," I said. But I made the same mistake I had made earlier. I forgot, just for a second, who I was talking to. Instead of looking my father straight in the eye, I looked down at my plate. When I looked up again, my father was staring at me. Mr. Hanover caught the look.

"If you know anything, Robyn," Mr. Hanover said, "or if you know anyone who might know anything, if you even just suspect that someone knows where she might be, I'd appreciate knowing." He looked at my father, who, in turn, looked at me.

"Robbie?"

"If anyone knows anything, they're not telling me," I said. And, because that was true — boy, was it ever! — I could meet my father's eyes and hold them while he searched for some clue. He sat back in his chair, and Mr. Hanover looked disappointed. My father kept his eyes steady on me. He didn't argue with me, he didn't push me anymore, but I knew that he wasn't one hundred percent satisfied with my answer.

"Maybe you should try the police again, Carl."

Mr. Hanover shook his head. "I thought about stopping by to see them on my way over here. But they just keep telling us the same thing — that she's old enough to leave school and to leave home, too, if that's what she wants."

"I still know a few people," my father said. He was being modest. He knows a lot of people. Cop people. "I'll get in touch, see if I can give them a nudge."

"I'd rather have you handle it, Mac," Mr. Hanover said. "So would Denise. She doesn't think the police are even interested. And after all the wild stories Trisha told them last time . . ." He sighed. "All I need to know is where I can find her so that I can at least try to talk to her."

"Of course," my father said. "If that's what you want." Then he said, "There's something I need your help with, Carl. I've been trying to get a meeting with Trevor Bailey."

Who was Trevor Bailey?

Mr. Hanover blinked. "Trevor? What do you want with Trevor?"

"I've been looking into the fire at the Doig place. I understand that he was the adjuster on that. You work with him, right?"

This was news. Mr. Hanover had some connection to the job my father was working on. Is that why Vern had given my father that look down in La Folie the first time my father had mentioned his name?

Mr. Hanover nodded.

"I'm looking into it for a client," my father said. "But I've hit a road block. Apparently your boss put the word out not to talk to me."

"I don't understand," said Mr. Hanover. "What is there to look into?"

"Trevor hasn't said anything to you about it, Carl, has he?"

"No," he said. "I haven't been at work much since Denise got sick again. What's going on, Mac? Are you saying that you don't think the fire was accidental? Because it was my understanding that the fire marshal said—"

"I need to talk to Trevor Bailey," said my father. "I need to ask him a few questions. I'd also like to know if he talked to Howie Maritz and, if he did, what Maritz said to him."

Mr. Hanover said he would see what he could do. Then he said he'd better get going. My father said "Just a minute," and got up and walked him to the door while I started clearing the dishes off the table. He stepped out into the hall with Mr. Hanover and stayed out there for a few minutes. I could hear them talking, but I couldn't make out what they were saying. When my father came back inside, he didn't ask me any more questions about Trisha. Instead, we cleaned up the kitchen together. He put some music on for us while we worked. When we finished, I glanced at my watch.

"I have to go, Dad," I said.

"I'd love to offer you a ride home, Robbie, but I kind of have plans . . ."

"It's okay, Dad," I said. I hadn't come to my father's place just to deliver the photos of Trisha. I had another reason for wanting to be in his neighbourhood. For that same reason, I didn't want my father to drive me home. Nor did I want to tell him where I was really going. "I'll take the bus," I said. "And anyway, I have to stop at Morgan's. I need to borrow some notes from her." This wasn't true, but it would help prevent him from changing whatever plans he had and driving me home instead.

"You sure you'll be okay?" he said.

I rolled my eyes. "You act like I've never gone home on my own before," I said. "Of course I'll be okay."

He kissed me on the top of my head and told me to be careful.

* * *

It was a fifteen-minute walk from my father's loft in the trendy part of what used to be a downscale neighbourhood to the high school in a part of the same neighbourhood that was still rundown. The lights were on in the school gymnasium. I headed across the parking lot toward it, thinking about what I was going to say when I got there. I'd been thinking about it all the way from my father's house — not just what I was going to say, but whether I should say anything at all. I guess that's why I didn't do the standard safety check that my father had taught me: Always be aware of who's on the street with you — front, back, and both sides. Always be aware if anyone is taking an interest in you. Always be aware of stores that are open and lights that are on in case you need help. Never let down your guard, especially after dark. Never go into isolated areas, like empty parking lots, at night.

I didn't even think about the safety check until I

heard something behind me. I turned and saw a car swing into the parking lot and advance toward me. I picked up my pace, walking quickly now toward the gym door. The car sped up. It was coming right at me. I doubled my pace. That's when I realized that I had done exactly the opposite of what my father had taught me. I had let down my guard. I had broken a few other rules, too. I was in a dark parking lot that had only two other cars in it. There were lights on in the gym, but they were shining through narrow windows set at the very top of a solid brick wall. I couldn't see what was happening inside and, for sure, no one inside — assuming there actually was someone in there — could see what was happening out in the parking lot. I realized, too, just how badly located the parking lot was. There were houses in the vicinity, but none of them overlooked the parking lot. My heart was racing, but it slammed to a stop when the car did a neat circle around me and pulled up between me and the gym door, blocking my path and almost blinding me with its headlights. The driver's door opened, but no light came on inside the car, so that as the driver got out, I didn't have a clear view of his face. When he stepped in front of the headlights, all I saw was an enormous, shadowy shape.

I should have listened to my father. At the very least, I should have told him the truth about where I was going.

Chapter Ten

My father says that nothing makes a bad situation worse than panic. So, he says, when you find yourself in a bad situation, the first thing you should do is take a deep breath. The second thing you should do is take stock. Figure out what you're up against. Think about it clearly. Then and only then can you make a rational decision about what to do.

I drew in a deep breath — and another and then another. I reviewed my situation. I was alone in a dark, deserted parking lot. I was face to face — well, face to shadowy figure — with a strange man whose intentions were unknown. What was the rational thing to do?

It turned out that my father's advice made sense. Forcing myself to breathe deeply and to think for a moment unfroze my brain. I remembered something else my father had told me: when you're in trouble, *real* trouble, yell, "Fire!" "Help" doesn't always get a reaction, he says, because too many people either think it's a joke or don't want to get involved. But everyone's afraid of fire, so *that* always gets people's attention — assuming anyone hears you.

I looked up at the lights twinkling out of the high-set gymnasium windows. They were all closed tight against the cool of the night, but still, if I screamed loudly enough . . . I opened my mouth.

"Robyn?" the shadowy figure said. He stepped a little to the side of the headlights so that I could see who it was.

"Mr. Hanover?" Geeze, after I had been thinking all those nice things about him. I had even felt sorry for him. And in return, he had scared me practically to death.

"I was driving by and I thought I saw you. I didn't mean to startle you," he said.

Startle? How about terrify?

"It's okay," I said, even though it wasn't.

"Look, I know you told your father that you didn't find out anything at school. But I'm not so old that I can't remember what it's like to be your age and to feel more solidarity with your peers than with your parents." I could see part of his face now. He looked the same as he had back at my father's place — worried, sad, and frightened. There was nothing at all scary about him. He reached into his pocket. "Trisha's mother wrote this last night," he said. He pulled out an envelope. "She's so worried and so sick. She can't sleep for all the worry. So she wrote Trisha a letter. I told her there was no way to get it to her, but she said she had to get things on paper. She had to tell Trisha how she feels. Now I'm thinking, well, if there's any chance at all that you can get this to her, I'd be so grateful. We both would be." He held the envelope out to me. "Take it," he said. "If you can't deliver it, fine. I understand. But her mother—" His voice broke. He turned his head away from me and raised a hand to his eyes. He was wiping away tears, I realized, and didn't want me to see. "Take it. Please. If you can get her to send a note back — or better yet, just to call home, so that we know she's all right — it would mean everything to her mother. If you see her, even if you can't get her to call home, you could let us know how she is."

I looked at the envelope in his hand.

"I don't know where she is," I said. And that was true. "I don't know how I could get it to her." Or maybe I did.

He was still holding the envelope out to me, like a piece of bright hope in an otherwise dark night.

"Even the slightest chance," he said.

I stepped forward and took it from him.

"Mr. Hanover, I really don't know if there's anything I can do."

"Thank you," he said, as if he hadn't heard me or maybe hadn't wanted to hear. "Thank you." He stood there for a moment and I thought he was going to say something else, but he didn't. He nodded at me and thanked me again in a quiet voice. Then he got into his car and drove away.

I stood in the darkness outside the gym for a moment, holding the envelope. Then I carried it over to the gym door and stepped inside to inspect it more closely. The envelope was cream-coloured, smooth, and heavy. It looked expensive. There was something besides paper inside. Something round and flat. I could feel it. I wondered what it was. I also wondered what the letter said. I tucked it into my backpack and pushed open the gym door. As soon as I did, I heard the *thump, thump, thump* of a basketball being dribbled. Then a roar filled the air. Basket, I thought. I peeked through the little round window in the inner gym door just as a whistle shrilled. Another roar went up from one end of the bleachers. Game over.

I looked along the bench for the coach of the winning team and found him — a smallish, balding man with a pink face and gold-rimmed glasses that were fastened behind his head with a band, I guess so they wouldn't come off as he ran alongside the court. He looked surprised to see me, but smiled and waved. When he finished talking to his team, he jogged over to me.

"Robyn, what are you doing here?" he said. He looked behind me, as if he were hoping to see someone with me. As if he were hoping to see my mother.

"Hi, Ted," I said. "I was in the neighbourhood."

He looked confused for a moment. Then he nodded. "Oh, I get it," he said. "Mac." Ted knew that my father lived in the area. To my mother's chagrin, Ted even likes my father. Ted is like that — he likes everyone.

"Can we talk?" I said.

He looked around again and still seemed disappointed that I was alone. "Sure, Robyn. As long as you don't mind waiting."

I said I didn't.

It took a few minutes for both teams to settle down and for everyone to shake hands. Then the players and coaches retreated to the locker room and the gym began to empty of spectators. By the time Ted reappeared in his street clothes, I was alone in the gym.

"How about I drive you home?" he said. "We can talk on the way." When I hesitated, he looked at me closely. He sighed and said, "I see."

"See what?"

"Your mother doesn't know you're here, does she?"

I shrugged.

"Okay," he said. "How about if I drive you *most of the way* home?"

I said sure and we went out into the parking lot together. For the first part of the drive, we talked about the basketball game — how it had gone, who was the best player on his team, what the team's chances were for the city championships, if it had any hope at all to make the regional playoffs. Finally Ted said, "How's your mother?"

I said she was okay.

He glanced at me. Maybe he wanted to see if I was telling the truth. Maybe he was trying to figure out what I knew.

"What happened, Ted?" I said.

"What do you mean?"

"Between you and Mom."

"I think your mother is the best person to ask about that."

"She won't tell me."

He shrugged. "Well, then—"

"Did you dump her, Ted?"

The car swerved a little. I grabbed at the dashboard while he straightened the steering wheel. "Is *that* what she told you?" he said.

"She didn't tell me anything. But I'm not blind. I can see she's upset. So I figured that must be what happened. I know it's none of my business, but—"

Ted stole another glance at me. He was taking extra care with his driving now. We passed street after street, covering a dozen or so blocks before he said, "I asked her to marry me."

If *I* had been driving, the car would have swerved again, probably right off the road and into a ditch. "Really?"

He looked pretty grim for a man who had just proposed marriage. Or maybe . . .

"She said no, huh?" I said.

"At first she said she'd have to think about it. Frankly, she looked stunned when I asked her. Not pleasantly surprised. Not even plain, old-fashioned surprised. More like I'd dropped a bomb on her." He shook his head. "I have to tell you, Robyn, it wasn't the reaction I'd hoped for. And since then—" He shrugged. "Since then I've talked to her secretary and left messages on her voice mail, but I haven't talked to her. Not that I haven't tried. She isn't returning my calls."

"Oh."

He glanced at me again. "So, how is she?"

I wasn't sure how to answer. "She said you two had decided to take a break from each other."

"A break?"

"I thought you must have dumped her, but that she didn't want to come right out and tell me."

I saw the flicker of a bitter smile on his lips and felt sorry for him.

"She's miserable, Ted."

He glanced at me as he digested what I had said. I think he was trying to look appropriately upset, but he was working hard to suppress a genuine smile. I had a pretty good idea what he was thinking. If she was miserable, that must mean she cared about him. Maybe it even meant that she was considering his proposal, because if she had already made up her mind and if the answer was no, if she had decided that she didn't love him, then why was she upset?

"I guess she needs time," he said. "Sometimes I forget."

"Forget what?"

"What she went through with your dad."

Oh. I looked out at familiar streets and houses. "You can drop me here, Ted."

* * *

My mother met me at the door. She said, "I tried to call you, but you must have shut off your cell phone again." She said, "I had to call your father to find out where you were." Then she said, "I also called Morgan."

Uh-oh. I'd forgotten to ask Morgan to cover for me. No wonder my mother had a pinched, worried look on her face. No wonder her arms were crossed over her chest.

"Where were you?" she said.

"I'm almost sixteen," I said, which, if you know anything at all about lawyers, was the absolute worst answer I could have given her. Lawyers are maniacs for precision. When they ask a question, they expect that question to be answered, not some other question. Lawyers do *not* appreciate evasion.

My mother's blue eyes narrowed to laser points. She said, "Where. Were. You."

"Mom, geeze, it's not like I disappeared off the face of the earth. I'm not a baby."

"Are you going to tell me where you were or am I going to have to ground you?"

Wait a minute! "Ground me? For what?"

"For lying to your father."

"If I lied to him, *he* should be the one to ground me."

"That can be arranged."

"Right. Like you would even bring yourself to have a conversation — *any* conversation — with him."

Her face changed, dramatically and instantly, from anger to shock to hurt to I don't even know what. But my mother is good at her job. She's been in court hundreds of times, and she's been handed a few nasty surprises. She always recovers. My father says she's quick on her feet.

"For the last time, are you going to tell me where you were?" she said.

"You're not the only person who has a private life, Mom."

"Fine. You're grounded for the weekend."

"Mom—"

"You want me to make it for a whole week?"

"That's not fair."

"Don't push me, Robyn."

Boy, was she in a bad mood! I thought about all the things I could have said, beginning with why she was divorced and running all the way through to how lucky I thought Ted was (at that exact moment, anyway) that she had declined his proposal (even though she hadn't actually come out and said no — yet). I glared at her, but I bit my tongue. If I could have cleared everything up by telling her exactly where I had been, maybe I would have done it. But I couldn't. If I told her the truth — especially now — she would get mad, probably even madder, for a different reason. I could just hear her: *How dare you talk to Ted behind my back. How dare you pry into my private life. How would you like it if I—*

I turned and went up to my room. I wanted to slam the door, but I held back. I dug my cell phone out of my pocket and called my father.

"Robbie, thank goodness," my father said. "Your mother called me — twice. She said you didn't go to Morgan's. She was worried when she couldn't get hold of you."

If she'd called my father, she really must have been beyond worried.

"I'm sorry, Dad."

"I hope you apologized to her, too."

I hadn't, but I didn't admit that.

"Look, Robbie, I know she's a little overprotective of you."

A little?

"In the future," my father said, "maybe you want to keep your phone on. You know, so she won't worry."

I told him okay. I added, "She grounded me for the whole weekend."

There was a moment of silence on the other end of the phone before he said, "You want me to talk to her?"

I knew that wouldn't make things better, so I said no. Then I said, "Dad? I ran into Mr. Hanover on the way home. He gave me a letter. He said if there was anything I could do to get it to Trisha, he'd appreciate it." No response. "Why would he do that, Dad? I already told him I didn't know anything."

More silence — hesitation? — then, "He's probably just hoping there's a chance you can." He didn't ask the next logical question. He didn't say, "Can you?"

So, just for the record, I said, "But I don't know anything."

"The man's desperate, Robbie. He told me that Denise has taken a turn for the worse and that it doesn't look good."

"What do you mean?"

"The cancer has spread, Robbie. I can't even begin to imagine how Carl feels." Then he told me he loved me. I noticed that, unlike my mother, he didn't demand to know where I had been. I concluded that he trusted me. I concluded that my mother didn't.

I stared at the ceiling for awhile. Then I called Morgan, whose first words were, "I screwed up. Sorry. When your mom asked for you, I should have said you were on your way home or in the bathroom or something. She took me by surprise. As soon as I thought about it, I tried to call you." Geeze, either I was going to have to live with the ring tone my father had chosen for my phone or I was going to have to change it. "Is everything okay?"

Funny she should ask. "You're not mad at *me*?" I said.

"Why should I be mad at you?"

I waited.

"Well, okay, I *was* mad at you," she said. "It was the way Billy looked at you. I thought you'd encouraged him. Then, after I calmed down, I thought, wait a minute, Robyn would never have put Billy up to asking me out. That was just Billy being needy."

"You think Billy's *needy*?" That was news to me. "He's your friend."

"You're my friend, too, but I don't want to go out with you, either."

"Are you saying you think *I'm* needy?"

I heard a long sigh on the other end of the line. "I'm

saying that friendship is one thing, chemistry is another."

Oh. "Have you talked to him?"

"Not yet."

"Are you going to?"

More silence, followed by another, deeper sigh. "I guess I should. I guess I owe him that. I probably could have handled it better, but he ambushed me."

"He didn't mean to. He was just nervous. Whatever you think of what he did, Morgan, he's still Billy."

"I know," she said. "I'll call him. I promise."

"Let me know if I need to administer emotional first aid — to either of you," I said.

It looked like tomorrow was going to be quite a day — and I hadn't even decided what I was going to do about the letter Mr. Hanover had given me.

Chapter Eleven

I lay in the dark, listening for my mother, wondering what she was doing, wondering if she would stop by my room on her way to bed to talk to me, maybe even (it was a stretch, I know) apologize to me. I heard the house grow quiet. I heard rustling as she came up the carpeted stairs. I heard silence as (I think) she paused outside my door. Then I heard the click of her bed-room door closing at the end of the hall and I felt angry all over again.

Eventually my thoughts drifted back to the letter Mr. Hanover had given me. I wondered what Trisha's mother had written. I wondered if it was something that Trisha would want to hear — *Honey, I love you, I miss you, I need you, whatever it is, please come home and we'll work it out, I know we will.* Or was it something that she wouldn't want to hear: *How dare you treat me like that, how dare you cause me all this worry, if you love me, you'll come home, if not . . .* I won-dered what kind of person Trisha's mother was and how she was facing her illness, especially now.

I wondered even more about Trisha. What kind of daughter takes off when her mother is so sick? What kind of daughter doesn't even call to say she's okay? Because let's say, for the sake of argument, that my mother married a guy I couldn't stand. Would I be so mad that I'd run away? If I left and then my mother got sick — as sick as a person could get — would I stay away? Would I be spiteful enough to make my already sick mother even sicker with worry? And if I did, what would that say about me?

And what about Mr. Hanover? Let's say, still for the sake of argument, that he wasn't the world's greatest stepfather. But Trisha's mother loved him — she married him, right? And obviously he cared enough about his wife to do everything he could to find Trisha or, at least, to get her to communicate with her mother so that she wouldn't worry so much. That had to earn him a few bonus points, didn't it?

I took the letter out of my backpack and turned it over and over in my hands. I wondered what else was in there. Some little token, I thought. Something her mother must have tucked inside for Trisha. But what? I thought about the electric kettle in the kitchen and the clouds of steam it produced when it boiled and how well steam works to loosen glue. Then I dropped the letter back into my backpack and thought some more.

* * *

The next morning when I woke up, I found a note at the kitchen table instead of my mother. *Early meeting,* it said in her neat, square printing. *Back by 8 p.m.* I gulped down some orange juice and packed my backpack. The envelope Mr. Hanover had given me was still inside. I decided to leave it there until I figured out what to do about it. I locked the house and set off for school.

Billy was waiting for me at the end of my street, his long, thin body half-draped around a lamppost, a solemn expression on his face. When I asked how he was, he said, "Do you ever wish you could go back in time?"

"Permanently, you mean? To live in a whole different era?" That would be one way to escape your problems.

"I mean, go back twenty-four hours," he said. "To relive one day without making a colossal mistake."

"Oh," I said. "Sure. I wish that all the time."

He fell into step beside me. "I blew it with Morgan."

"I wouldn't say that."

"She hates me, Robyn."

"She likes you — as a *friend*."

"That's just what every guy wants to hear."

"Maybe there's no chemistry," I said.

"You mean, there's no chemistry for her." He trudged in silence beside me for a few blocks. "Robyn? I think I'm in love with her."

"Billy, I don't know what to say."

"What's wrong with me? Why doesn't she like me?"

"She —"

"I mean, why doesn't she like me as more than a friend?"

"I don't know what to say, Billy. But she's still your friend. That means something, doesn't it?"

He nodded glumly. "You're lucky, Robyn. You've got Nick."

Right.

I got through the day. I even got through a pop quiz in history, although I wouldn't have bet much on getting a decent grade. The whole time I was thinking about the letter Mr. Hanover had given me, about what I should do with it, about who could help me.

I left school the minute the bell rang and headed across town to Somerset. I got there in time to see some of the guys who lived there coming back from school. I recognized one of them at the same time that he recognized me.

"Hey, Antoine." I hadn't seen him since the summer. He didn't go to the same school as Nick. He smiled when he saw me, though.

"You looking for Nick?" he said.

I nodded.

"He went to a meeting with his social worker and Ed."

Antoine is tall, like Nick, but bulkier, with close-cut hair and big clothes. He has light chocolate skin and stunning blue eyes. I didn't like him when I first met him. The feeling was mutual. Now I think he feels better about me, but that doesn't make it easy to read what's going on behind those eyes of his. My father has a theory about guys like Antoine. He says they've been disappointed one time too many, so now they hide whatever they're feeling. Most of the time they act like they don't care what happens, because if they don't care, they can't be disappointed again. That means that if you want to know what's going on with Antoine, you have to ask, and then it's a toss-up whether or not you get an answer.

My question of the day: "Is everything okay with Nick?"

And there it was, the straight-on blank look. "What do you mean?" What he really meant was, *How much do you know?*

"I met Glen," I said. "I know he's a cop."

Antoine's face relaxed a little, but he shook his head. "You know I can't talk about Nick. It's up to him what gets said about him."

"I don't want you to talk about him. I just want to know whether you think he's going to get out of here in a couple of weeks like he's supposed to, whether he's going to go home."

"I think he's going to get out of here okay," Antoine said. "But home?" He shrugged. "What's home, anyway?"

Good question. "Do you know when he's going to be back?"

He shook his head. "I gotta go. I gotta be inside."

I watched him shamble up the walk to the front door and disappear inside. I retreated half a block to the bus stop. There was a bench there and I dropped down onto it to wait. It was a beautiful autumn day.

The foliage on the oak and maple trees that lined the street had already started turning red and orange and yellow. Halfway up the block, a man was raking leaves on his front lawn. Across the street, some kids were playing ball in a small park. Down the other way another man sat in a grey car, reading a newspaper. Although Somerset was located in a residential neighbourhood, it was on a bus route, so there was a fair amount of traffic. I turned my head every time I heard a car coming. It was nearly an hour before I saw one that I recognized. When it made the turn into the driveway at Somerset, I walked toward it.

"Hello, Robyn," Mr. Jarvis said as he got out of the car. He sounded surprised and not surprised both at the same time.

I said hi and then turned my attention to Nick, who was getting out of the passenger side.

"Well," Mr. Jarvis said. He looked from me to Nick. "I can trust you to come inside when you're finished out here, right, Nick?"

Nick was staring at me. He was trying to look cool, trying to give me an Antoine blank-look, but he wasn't succeeding. Nick isn't like Antoine. He doesn't always like to say what's going on in his head, but, boy, does he ever have trouble hiding his feelings.

"Yeah," he said to Mr. Jarvis. "I'll be right in."

Mr. Jarvis went inside. I circled around to where Nick was standing. At first he wouldn't look at me. Then he slipped a hand in mine.

"I went back to the coffee shop to look for you," he said. "You were gone."

"I waited for half an hour."

"I'm sorry. But Beej is . . . emotional, you know?" I didn't know and I couldn't say I even cared, but I held my tongue. "I had to get her calmed down."

"How are you getting along with your aunt?" I said.

The question seemed to confuse him. "My aunt?"

"You're supposed to go and live with her in two more weeks, right?"

He looked down the driveway to the road. "I've been thinking maybe I'd do something else."

"Yeah? Like what?"

He shrugged, like it was no big deal. "Maybe a group home."

"You're in a group home now," I said. "You've been telling me ever since I met you that you can't wait to get out."

"That's different," he said. "I'm *here* because I have to be. I'm talking about a different kind of place, you know, where a bunch of kids live together and someone runs the place, but there aren't so many rules."

"You think you'd like that?"

He shrugged again.

"You think you'd like it better than living with your aunt?"

He looked directly at me. "I think it would be good for me."

"Because of Glen?"

"Come on, Robyn—"

"I really like you, Nick," I said. "I care what happens to you. But you always act like you don't trust me."

He looked at me for a long time. For a while, his face was hard and his nostrils flared out. Then his breathing got quieter and he shook his head.

"If I live with my aunt, something bad is going to happen," he said. "She's crazy about Glen, but he doesn't want me around. I don't like him and he doesn't like me. And whenever he gets mad, which he does every time I go there, she gets mad, too. At me. She tells me to behave myself. Don't do things that annoy Glen. She says she's tired of being alone and she really likes him and she wants it to work out between them. If I go to live there, she's only going to end up sorry she ever said I could stay there in the first place. Anyway, I bet Glen will eventually fix it so she throws me out. But if I go and live someplace else, maybe she'll still be my aunt, maybe I can see her from time to time, and maybe she'll still like me." When he looked at me, I had no trouble reading the hurt on his face. "I don't want her to hate me, Robyn."

I slipped my arms around his waist. He didn't pull away. After a while, he wrapped his good arm around me and held me close. His chin rested lightly on my head. It felt good.

"Nick?"

"Mmm?"

I liked how warm I felt pressed up against his

chest. I like that he sounded so content, like a cat purring. I was sorry that I was probably going to mess it all up.

"Trisha's father gave me a letter. Trisha's mother wrote it. He asked me if there was any way I could get it to Trisha."

I felt him go rigid.

"What did you tell him?" he said.

"Nothing."

He pulled away from me. "Then why did he give you a letter for her?"

"I told him when he gave it to me that I didn't think there was anything I could do. I didn't tell him anything else. How could I? I don't *know* anything." He kept staring at me. "But I think Kenny does and so does Beej."

He stepped away from me, his eyes cold again.

"Come on, Nick. Trisha's mother is really sick. She just wants to know that Trisha is okay. All I want to do is give her the letter. That's all. Give it to her and let her decide what to do about it." Then, because it didn't look like he was going to offer, I had to come right out and say it. "I need your help."

"This has nothing to do with me. It has nothing to do with you, either."

"She's in my history class," I said.

"Yeah? So?" He was really angry now.

"So we were working on a project together. But she didn't get a lot done, probably because her mother is so sick. I could have been nice about it, but I wasn't." I told him what had happened. He was looking at me strangely. Maybe he was having trouble picturing me being a total bitch. I couldn't make myself meet his eyes. "That same day, she took off."

"That's the personal reason, huh?"

I looked up at him.

"In the restaurant," he said, "before Beej showed up. You said you had a personal reason for wanting to find her. That's it?"

I nodded. "I think Kenny Merchant might have some idea where she is. And I *know* Beej knows something. I was looking right at her when she saw Trisha's photograph. I saw the look on her face. That's why she ran out of the coffee shop, isn't it? And why you had to take so long calming her down? She thought you were going to tell me something."

He kept looking at me. "I don't know where she is."

"But Beej knows, doesn't she?"

He said nothing.

"I could have told my father," I said. "But I didn't. I haven't said a word to him." *Yet.* "I know you think it's none of my business, and maybe you're right. But I feel bad about what I did. You think it's up to Trisha to decide what she wants to do. I agree with you. But, Nick, I feel sorry for her mother, too. That's why I want to deliver the letter to Trisha — so Trisha can see for herself how her mother feels and she can decide for herself what she wants to do. I'll meet her anywhere she wants."

"And maybe while you're delivering it, you could apologize to her, is that it?"

I felt my cheeks redden. "Maybe," I said.

"Hey, Robyn?"

I looked up at him again.

"Do you really think someone would run away and stay away this long just because you said something stupid?"

"Everyone says she takes off whenever she's upset or angry."

He didn't look convinced.

"Even if I'm only partly responsible, I want to apologize," I said. "All I'm asking you to do is ask Beej."

He shook his head. "It's none of my business."

"Have you talked to Trisha?"

"I've never even met her," he said. "I don't want to get involved."

"Can't you just ask Beej? Please?"

"And if she says no, what are you going to do? Tell your dad? Get him to go after her, even though you have no real idea what's going on and why Trisha ran away?"

I looked down the street, at the nice, peaceful neighbourhood. The man who had been raking his lawn before was now carrying paper bags of leaves out to the curb for pick-up. The kids who had been playing ball were goofing around on the swings. The guy who had been sitting in his car reading the paper was still sitting, still reading.

"I'll make you a deal," Nick said finally. "I'll ask Beej — *ask* her, that's all — if she'll give your message to Trisha. If she won't, that's the end of it. If she says she knows where Trisha is and can deliver the message, then it's up to Trisha what happens after that. Okay, Robyn? It's up to *her*, not you. And you have to promise that no matter what she says, you won't tell your dad anything, not about Trisha, not about Beej, not about Kenny. Deal?"

His purple eyes searched mine while I thought it over. What if Trisha refused? And what if it turned out that Beej knew where she was? Could I really keep that information from my father? Would it be the right thing to do?

Someone called Nick's name. It was Mr. Jarvis, standing in the door to Somerset. Nick waved at him and said he'd be right there. Then he looked back at me, wanting my answer.

"Deal," I said.

Chapter Twelve

I arrived home about five minutes before my mother. She looked tired when she came through the door. She set down her bulging briefcase, dropped her keys in the bowl on the little table in the front hall, shrugged out of her jacket and hung it in the hall closet. I stood in the door to the kitchen, where I had been checking the fridge for supper possibilities, and watched her kick off her shoes. I waited to see if she was going to apologize for the night before or, at the very least, relent on grounding me. But all she said was, "Have you eaten yet?"

"I was just going to make myself a sandwich," I said.

"Good. Because I don't feel like cooking. I'm going to take a bath."

Another bath? My mother was normally one of those people who didn't feel right unless she was spending every minute of her day doing something productive. Taking baths was for when she was (a) dead tired or

(b) depressed. She had taken a lot of very long baths when she and my father were breaking up and then when they separated. There had been a pattern then. Bath, then robe and head towel, then ice cream.

She climbed halfway up the stairs, turned, and said, "You're still grounded."

Okay, she was in that kind of mood. I went into the kitchen. I was making my sandwich when my father called.

"Cheer up, Robbie," he said when I told him what my mother had said. "It's only one weekend. When you're sprung, we'll do something fun, okay?"

I said okay. I hung up and finished making my sandwich. I was taking the first bite when Morgan called.

"I talked to Billy," she said.

"And?"

I heard a long sigh. "*And* I told him that I really like him — *as a friend*. When I said that, he turned bright red, you know, the way he does." Red like Christmas ribbon. Like cherry lollipops. "We're going to a movie tomorrow. You know, like buddies. I don't suppose you want to come and help make sure that Billy understands?"

"I'd love to," I said. "But I can't. I'm grounded." I told her what had happened. "Don't worry," I said. "I'm pretty sure he understands."

"He's a sweet guy," she said. "I just don't want to go out with him."

I told her, "Have fun."

"Right," she said. "And you be good." As if I could

be anything else, stuck in the house all weekend.

My mother stopped by my room after her bath. She said she was sorry she had to ground me. *Had* to. She said it was the only way she could think of to make sure I knew she was serious. For a moment, I thought she was going to say it was for my own good. Thankfully, she didn't.

She was at my door again first thing the next morning, dressed in a business suit even though it was Saturday morning. She had to go to the office, she said. Then she had to meet with a client.

"I'll check in with you," she said.

"Okay. But don't freak out if I don't answer the phone. Try me on my cell, okay?" My mother's eyes narrowed. She looked suspiciously at me. Thanks a lot, Mom. "I'm stuck here all day, right?" In fact, all weekend. "With nothing to do, right? I figured it would be a perfect time to clean out the garage." Her eyes got even narrower. "There's no phone in the garage, so if you call me, I won't be able to hear you. You'll have to get me on my cell." When she finally nodded, I said, "You're welcome."

"Thank you," she said.

I absolutely intended to spend the day doing what I had promised to do. I even made it out to the garage. I was standing in the little square of clear space in the middle of it, trying to figure out where to start — and whether this was going to turn out to be the never-ending chore — when *Ta-DA, Ta-DA, Ta-da-da-da-da-da-DA.* I rolled my eyes. There was nothing like motherly trust.

Except it wasn't my mother.

It was Nick.

"She said okay," he said.

"Beej?"

"She said Trisha wants the letter from her mother. So come and meet me. I'm downtown at the drop-in centre. I'll be outside. I've got the dogs." He meant the dogs from his Saturday dog-walking job.

I hesitated. I could have told him it would have to wait until Monday — because I was grounded. Or I could just go and do it. With luck — no, with good planning — I'd be back well before my mother returned home and I'd still have time to make progress on the garage. And if she called to check on me, well, she was going to call my cell. She'd never know I'd been away from home.

"Hey, Robyn? You still there?"

I said I was.

"Beej says if you want to do it, you have to come right now."

I said I'd be there as soon as I could. After I hung up, I closed the garage door, stuffed the envelope Mr. Hanover had given me into my bag, and headed for the nearest bus stop. As I hurried down the street, I checked out the neighbours' houses to see if anyone my mother knew was outside doing yard work or maybe getting into a car to go somewhere — anybody who might see me and might mention it to my mother, so then I could say, yes, well, at around such-and-such a time I ran down to the store for some more garbage bags (note to self: buy garbage bags on the way home) or, better yet, rubber gloves (note to self: forget garbage bags, buy rubber gloves) because you wouldn't believe all the gunk that collected under Dad's workbench, the one he never used. So, yeah, I know I was grounded, but it was just a quick trip to the store and, believe me, it wasn't any fun.

I got lucky. Our street was quiet for a Saturday morning. I saw Mrs. Giles come out her side door and head around to the back of her house. I don't think she saw me. I saw a shabby-looking guy come down from the Rivards' porch, cut across their lawn, trudge up the Carlings' front steps, shove a handful of flyers into their letter box, and then cut across the Carlings' lawn to the house next door. I saw a car sitting near the end of the Bellagios' driveway, but it wasn't Mr. or Mrs. Bellagios' car. They drove his and hers midnight blue Renaults. This was a beat-up old grey car with a guy in it wearing mirrored aviator sunglasses that were seriously out of date. He seemed to be checking out something on a clipboard. I figured he was some kind of salesman. Or maybe a utility consumption inspector, you know, a meter reader. Other than that, there wasn't a soul around.

I got lucky with the bus, too. One came along almost as soon as I reached the bus stop. Nick was waiting for me on the sidewalk outside the drop-in centre. There were two big dogs with him. His left arm was still in a sling, so he was holding their leashes awkwardly with his right hand. I knew both dogs. One was a black mammoth named Orion, whom Nick had helped to train at the animal shelter over the summer. The other was a German shepherd named Bunny. The name was someone's idea of a joke, I guess, because Bunny did not look even remotely cute or bunny-like. Nick had told me more than once that they were really pussycats and that there was no way they would ever hurt me. It didn't help much. Dogs make me nervous. Big dogs scare me.

"Come on," Nick said.

We hadn't gone more than two steps when *Ta-DA, Ta-DA, Ta-da-da-da-da-da-DA*. Nick's head whipped around as he tried to locate the source of the music.

"My cell phone," I said. "Don't ask."

I dug in my bag for my phone, and then I panicked. We were standing on a busy downtown street. Traffic sounds swirled around me. Whoever was on the other end of the phone — for example, my mother — would hear those sounds and know that Dorothy wasn't in Kansas anymore. I glanced around and spotted a discount bookstore that looked almost deserted.

"I'll be right back," I said to Nick. I stepped inside the store and answered my cell, doing my best to ignore the troll-like man glowering at me from behind the cash register.

"Oh, hi, Mom," I said. "Sure, I'm fine. There's a lot more stuff in here than I thought. I don't know if I'm going to be able to get it all finished in one day." Might as well prepare her for a less-than-spic-and-span garage when she got home.

My mother sounded mellower now than she had

when she'd left the house. She said not to worry, whatever I didn't get done today, I could do tomorrow. She said she'd be home by six. She said we'd order pizza and maybe she'd pick up some videos we could watch together. In other words, in her own way, she finally apologized.

By the time I finished my call and went back outside, Nick was pacing impatiently on the sidewalk.

"Beej is going to think we're not coming," he said. He nudged me with his sore arm. I followed him and the dogs down the street, around a few corners and then hesitated when he stepped into an alley. The way I see it, downtown alleys are like winter nights — long, dark, and lonely. They're littered with garbage dumpsters and garbage that hasn't made it into dumpsters. They're probably crawling with rats (although I had never actually seen one, thank goodness). And the only people you ever see in alleys are strange people, homeless people, crazy people, and people who are doing things they don't want anyone to see.

"Come on," Nick said. When I didn't follow him immediately, he said, "It's okay, Robyn. I'd never let anything happen to you." He looked down at the dogs. "Neither would Orion or Bunny."

I stuck close to Nick while trying to keep my distance from the dogs.

The alley turned out to be the entrance to a whole network of alleys that ran behind and around stores, restaurants, and office towers. Nick led me through it as if he were guiding me through his own house, which made me wonder. I thought I knew a lot about Nick. But I obviously didn't know everything. For example, I didn't know how he had managed to acquire an intimate knowledge of downtown back alleys.

Finally Beej and her bulging backpack appeared from behind a dumpster. She looked all around, frowning, as she checked to make sure that I hadn't been followed. It didn't seem to make any difference when Nick told her that it was all good, she could trust me. Her eyes darted here and there, taking in every inch of the alley. She thrust out her hand.

"Give me the letter," she said.

"I'd like to give it to Trisha myself," I said.

Beej's small dark eyes got smaller. Her suspicious look grew even more suspicious. "I knew there was going to be a catch," she said. "Look, Trisha wants the letter, but she doesn't want to see you. She doesn't like you and she doesn't trust you. Okay?"

It wasn't exactly okay and, besides, "I'd like to give it to her in person," I said, "so I can tell her parents that she's all right. Her mother is also hoping that she'll send back a note, you know, since she hasn't called home or anything since she left."

Beej gave me a funny look. She shook her head. "If you want her to get that letter, you have to give it to me. If you don't want to give it to me, fine, we're done here."

I looked pleadingly at Nick, but all he did was shrug. He wasn't going to help, and Beej wasn't going to budge.

"Okay," I said. "How about if Nick goes with you? He can see how Trisha is and he can tell me. Then I can tell her parents."

Beej's look of suspicion turned to one of contempt. "What's the matter?" she said. "Don't you trust me to tell you the truth?"

"Do *you* trust *me*?" I said.

She smiled, but there was nothing light-hearted about the expression. "Sure, okay," she said, just like that, without any hesitation. "Nick can come." Because, of course, she trusted him.

Nick handed me the dog leashes and took the letter. He stuck it in his pocket and squeezed my hand.

"Stay here with the dogs, okay?" he said. "I'll be back as soon as I can."

I looked doubtfully at the two animals and even more doubtfully around the litter-strewn alley.

"Orion won't let anyone mess with you," Nick said.

I looked at the big black dog. He had terrified me the first time I met him and, to be honest, he still scared me. But he was used to me even if I wasn't used to him. And Nick had complete faith in him. So I nodded. When Nick and Beej walked down the alley together and disappeared around a corner, I moved closer to the dumpster. Dogs or no dogs, I didn't want anyone who might see me standing deep in an alley, far, far from the bustle of the street, to get any ideas.

As I stepped back, Orion tensed and strained

against his leash. It took a moment before I saw why. Up ahead, a man in a dark suit cut across the alley. Orion pulled toward him, and I had to keep a firm grip on his leash to stop him from bolting. If the man had come my way, I would never have been able to hold Orion. Thank goodness he had headed somewhere else. In fact, he had gone in the same direction as Nick and Beej.

And he was wearing aviator sunglasses.

The man in the beat-up old grey car in front of the Bellagios' this morning had been wearing aviator sunglasses. The man sitting in the car near Somerset yesterday hadn't been, but his car had been old and grey, just like the one outside the Bellagios'. He'd sat there for a long time. He'd been sitting there while I waited for Nick and he'd still been sitting there later when I was talking to him — more than an hour in total.

Was it the same man?

If it wasn't, what was a man in a suit doing in an alley, and why had he gone in the same direction as Nick and Beej?

I shook my head. This wasn't cloak-and-dagger spy stuff. This was Trisha who had run away from home. And, okay, in the movies or on TV, when you see a guy in mirrored sunglasses parked in a car like that, you think, he's watching someone. But this wasn't the movies. This was real life — a real-life case of a guy who had asked my father to look for a girl who had run away. My father, who was very good at what he did. My father, who knew that Mr. Hanover had given me the letter. My father, who hadn't been one hundred percent satisfied that I was telling him the truth. Who had spoken out in the hall to Mr. Hanover about an hour before Mr. Hanover suddenly appeared in the high-school parking lot with the letter. Who was known for doing whatever it took to finish a job. Who had been known to resort to subterfuge, like sending someone undercover as a maid to grab two children who had been kidnapped by their own father. What had Mr. Hanover said that first time I'd met him in my father's loft? *The end justifies the means, right, Mac?* I wondered about the letter Mr. Hanover had given me. I thought about when he had given it to me. I also thought about why — and wondered if maybe the letter wasn't the point at all. Then I started to get angry.

I tied the dog leashes to a disgustingly sticky bar that ran along the side of the dumpster. Then I ran down the alley to look for the man in the aviator sunglasses.

When I reached the corner where Nick and Beej had disappeared, I stopped and peeked around carefully. No Nick. No Beej. No man. I rounded the corner and ran quietly along the alley until I reached a street. The alley continued on the other side, and I saw someone moving stealthily down it, away from me. Someone in a dark suit. I crossed the street and hung back in the mouth of the alley until the man turned left.

When I reached the corner where he had turned, I hung back again. I peeked around cautiously and saw him, moving quietly and steadily, not looking back because, well, why should he? As far as he was concerned, he was the follower.

I kept a steady pace behind him as we moved east and then south into an area of the city that was filled with housing projects and homeless shelters. The streets became progressively more rundown and were lined with bargain outlets, charity second-hand stores, and pawnshops. The alleys weren't as deserted in this part of town, and now I wished I had brought Orion and Bunny with me. A toothless old man gazed up at me through glazed eyes as I went by. A couple of young, tough-looking guys regarded me with more interest. I scurried past them and kept moving until I saw the man in the aviator sunglasses disappear into what looked like an abandoned building. The windows on the first couple of floors were boarded over and the outside brickwork was covered with graffiti. I peeked around the corner and watched the man push a loose board aside and step into the building. Beej and Nick must have gone in there. I glanced around, but didn't see anyone. I approached the building cautiously and let myself in the same way as the man in the sunglasses had.

It was dark inside. The only light — and there wasn't much — came down from the stairwell from the grimy windows on the third floor. Garbage — fast food wrappers, pop cans, candy bar wrappers and things that I didn't even want to think about much less have to look at — littered the floor. The air was sharp and foul smelling and reminded me of the time we set up camp too close to an outhouse. I stood there, breathing through my mouth and trying not to gag, while I strained to listen. Nothing. No, wait a minute, a murmur. Up above. Voices? Beej? Nick? Trisha? What about the man in the sunglasses? Where was he?

I started up the stairs, which were also littered with food wrappers, pop cans, and bottles, and . . . Something skittered on the stairs just where I was about to put one sneakered foot. I clapped a hand over my mouth to stifle the scream that was rising in my throat. Was that what I thought it was? Was it a rat? It looked as big as a cat, but, boy, I had never seen a cat with a tail like that. Geeze, and where there was one rat . . .

I stood there, frozen, until the skittering stopped. I swallowed my terror — at least, I *tried* to — as I tip-toed up the stairs and headed toward the low hum of a male voice. At first I thought it must be Nick, but when I peeked around a corner, I saw the man in the dark suit, his sunglasses tucked into his jacket pocket now. He was talking softly into a cell phone. Then he shut off the phone and started silently down the hall. I pulled back, in case he turned around. When I peeked out again, he was opening a door at the end of the hall. As he shouldered his way through it, I heard a shout, followed by a scream. I ran down the hall toward the door.

When I got there, I saw that the man in the dark suit had Trisha by the arm. Nick was all over the guy, trying to wrench Trisha free. Beej was holding the envelope and a piece of paper — the letter, I guessed — and was grabbing at something — at Trisha's purse, it looked like. She turned and stared at me when I came into the room. So did Trisha. She looked accusingly at me. Nick hit the man in the dark suit. He staggered back, still holding tight to Trisha. Trisha let out a scream. I saw the man's hand curl into a fist and he lashed out, punching Nick hard in the belly. I was glad he was holding onto Trisha because the man looked angry and I had the feeling that if he'd let go of her, he'd have gone at Nick with both fists swinging. As it was, all the air went out of Nick with an *oomph* and he sank to his knees, doubled over.

Next I heard footsteps thundering up the stairs behind me. Then I heard them at the end of the hall pounding closer and closer. Suddenly, two men burst into the room. One of them was Carl Hanover. He surveyed the scene inside quickly.

"Trisha," he said. "Thank goodness."

Trisha's eyes widened when she saw him. She struggled even harder.

Mr. Hanover turned to me. "Robyn," he said. "I can't thank you enough for finding her. These men are friends of mine. I asked them to come with me, to help me make sure that Trisha gets home safely." He turned to Trisha. "It's time to come home," he said.

Beej's eyes got harder and colder. Nick was still on his knees, one hand on the floor to steady himself. He looked up at me, his face filled with bitter disappointment. Trisha struggled. Beej dove in, grabbing at Trisha's purse again, yanking it as if she thought she could use it to pull Trisha away from the men. One of the men turned and shoved Beej, sending her reeling. She lost her balance and crashed to the floor.

"Gently, please," Mr. Hanover said to the man. "These kids were only trying to help Trisha." He turned to Beej. "Isn't that right?"

Beej scowled at him. Mr. Hanover didn't seem to notice. "Come on, Trisha," he said. "I have a car outside. Your mother is so worried."

Trisha kicked out at him. Mr. Hanover nodded at the man in the dark suit and the other man. They were both holding Trisha. She was still struggling, but not as much now.

"Don't let them take me away!" she said, her voice shrill. "Please." She was looking at Beej and Nick, not at me, when she said it.

"Let's get you home before your mother suffers any more," Mr. Hanover said.

"What have you done to her?" Trisha said.

"What have *I* done to her?" Mr. Hanover said. "Your disappearing act has put her in the hospital."

"The hospital?" Trisha said, her voice small and weak now. She glanced at me as she was led to the door. She didn't seem angry at me any more. Instead, there was a different expression on her face.

Beej ran at the two men holding her.

"Hey, wait a minute," she yelled, grabbing at Trisha's purse again. One of the men turned to Mr. Hanover, who shook his head. The man pushed Beej firmly aside and the two of them escorted Trisha from the room, half-carrying, half-dragging her.

Mr. Hanover squeezed my shoulder. "Thank you, Robyn," he said. "Denise will be so grateful. I won't say that she's blind to Trisha's behaviour, especially the way she's always running away and the crazy stories she tells. But you know how mothers are. They love their children no matter what."

"My dad told me about your wife," I said. "I'm sorry. I hope she's going to be okay." It sounded lame, I know. But it was all I could think of to say.

Nick struggled to his feet and staggered to the door. For a moment I thought he was going to go after Trisha. Then, *smack.* My cheek stung from the force of Beej's hand. She glared at me, her eyes filled with venom.

"Trisha was right about you," she said.

"Robyn—" Mr. Hanover said.

"I'm okay," I told him. "Really."

He hesitated a moment before leaving the room. After he had gone, I turned to Beej. "I didn't know this was going to happen," I said.

Beej glared at me again. "Nick says you're smart, but for a smart girl, you sure don't know much. You led them right to her." She thrust the envelope at me. "*Letter,*" she snorted. "Did you even look inside?"

"No, of course not," I said.

Beej rolled her eyes and looked at Nick. "You're actually going out with her?" she said.

"Look, I know you're Trisha's friend," I said.

"*Friend?*" She looked at me as if I were insane. "I'm not her friend. That girl has too many problems to be my friend."

170

"Then why did you just slap me?"

"Because, thanks to you, some valuable stuff of mine just walked out the door."

"What are you talking about?"

"Trisha. She's got my stuff in her bag." So that's why Beej had been grabbing for Trisha's purse. "She has stuff that belongs to me and now I'll probably never get it back."

She thrust the envelope and the piece of paper at me before stomping out of the room.

I looked at the paper. It was blank on both sides. Baffled, I turned to Nick.

"The envelope," he said, still gasping for breath.

I looked in the envelope. When Mr. Hanover first gave it to me, I had felt something inside. I could see it now, a small, flat, round disc. But what was it? I tipped it out into my hand, looked at it again, and then turned to Nick.

"Tracking device," Nick said. "Bet you anything."

I stared at it and thought again about my father talking to Mr. Hanover out in the hallway.

"Where are the dogs?" Nick said, his voice flat, as if he blamed me for what had happened.

"Back in the alley where you left me," I said. "Nick, honest, I had no idea—"

My phone trilled. While I fumbled for it, Nick headed for the door.

"Nick, wait."

My phone trilled again and Nick kept right on going. I pushed the talk button and said hello. I saw Nick start down the stairs at the same time as I heard my mother say, "Robyn, where are you? And don't tell me you're in the garage, because I was just there."

If things are going to go bad, they might as well go all the way, I thought. Now I was in trouble — *big* trouble — with my mother. I figured that was the worst it could get.

I was wrong.

"Mom, I—"

"Robyn, do you know where the General Hospital is?"

"Yeah, sure, but—"

"Meet me there. In Emergency."

"Why? Mom, what's going on?"

"Your father's there," she said. "He's hurt."

"Hurt? What's wrong?"

"I don't know yet. Just meet me there, Robyn."

Chapter Thirteen

I didn't think about rats on the way down the stairs. I didn't think about how angry I was that my father had probably helped Mr. Hanover to trick me. Instead, I thought: hurt how? And how badly? I ran down the stairs into the gloom below, panicked for a moment until I got my bearings and found the loose board, squeezed out of the garbage dump of a building, and raced down the alley to the nearest street. When I got there, I started waving frantically, desperate to flag down a taxi. I didn't even think about money until I was in the back seat and the taxi was making its way through midday Saturday traffic to the hospital. I rummaged in my purse, worried that I wouldn't have enough to pay the driver. I started to panic again, imagining the taxi driver locking me inside the car and calling the cops while my father was inside the hospital, in Emergency. It turned out I needn't have worried. Henri St-Onge was standing outside the emergency entrance. She dashed over to the taxi as soon as it pulled up and thrust some money at the driver.

"Your mother's inside," she said, opening the door for me. "Come on."

Henri (short for Henrietta) is Vern's girlfriend. She's small and round and has a quirky, totally unique wardrobe. She's an artist.

"What happened?" I asked her. "Is my dad okay?"

"I don't know. The police called, looking for Vern, but he's up north on a job. He won't be able to get a flight back until late tonight. They told me your father had been pretty badly beaten up. He was unconscious." I swallowed hard. Unconscious wasn't good. Unconscious could mean a serious injury. "They told me they'd called an ambulance and that he was on his way to the hospital. They asked who they should notify, so I told them your mother." She looked a little worried. "I hope I did the right thing. She seems pretty shook up, considering." Considering a three-year separation and a year-old divorce, she meant.

She was right. My mother's face was pinched and pale, and her eyes were watery, as if she had been crying. Was that possible?

"Mom, have you heard anything?" I said. "Is he going to be okay?"

"I haven't been able to get any information yet," my mother said. She sounded angry. "They keep telling me they'll let me know as soon as there's any news."

"I'll go and ask again," Henri said. She bustled away.

I sat down next to my mother.

"I'm not even going to ask why you weren't where you were supposed to be," she said, still angry. It was hard to tell, though, if she was angry with me or just angry in general. Probably both.

"Henri said he was beaten up," I said. "She said—" I didn't mean for those tears to start dribbling down my cheek. Nor did I mean for my lips to start trembling, but they did.

My mother slipped an arm around me and held me tight. "Once when you were just a baby, your father got a call. It was a bar fight. Most people break it up when the police arrive. But there were a couple of guys who were too drunk, I guess. One of the guys came at your father with a bar stool. Your father ended up with a broken nose and a broken jaw. He was unconscious for hours. I was really scared. But he bounced right back. Your father's like that, Robyn." Even so, I could tell she was worried, too.

Henri came back with a man in a suit. The man smiled at my mother.

"Patricia," he said. "It's been a while."

"Hello, Jim," she said.

Jim looked at me. "You can't possibly be Robyn," he said.

"Robyn, this is Detective Harwood."

"Actually, it's Detective Sergeant now," Detective Sergeant Harwood said. "I used to work with your father."

"What happened, Jim?" my mother said.

Detective Sergeant Harwood sat down. "We won't

know for sure until we can talk to Mac. He was found in an old industrial park. His wallet is missing. His car isn't anywhere in the vicinity. We don't know whether he was out there for some reason or if he was taken there. We don't know if it was a mugging or a carjacking or if it was something else. About the only thing we do know is that he's lucky a security car that patrols the area drove by when it did. The two guys who were beating up Mac took off. The guard didn't see where they went or whether they had Mac's car. He called it in and stayed to give first aid to Mac."

"What do you mean, you don't know if it was something else?" my mother said.

"It's possible it was related to something he's working on. Vern says he's been looking into that fire up at the Doig place."

My mother did not look pleased. "And to think I used to worry about him when he was with the police," she said.

"We're going to find out what happened, Patricia," Detective Sergeant Harwood said. "Don't worry."

But we did worry. And the longer we waited there, the more we worried. It seemed like forever before a woman wearing scrubs and a white lab coat came over to talk to my mother.

"Mrs. Hunter?" she said.

"It's Ms Stone," my mother said. "We're divorced. This is our daughter Robyn." Then, sounding like someone who wasn't even remotely divorced, she said, "How is he?"

The woman sat down beside my mother. "He's suf-fered a concussion. He also has a ruptured spleen and a couple of cracked ribs." My mother's face went pale. I bit my lip to keep from crying. "We have everything more or less under control. His condition isn't critical," the doctor said, "but it is serious. We're going to keep him here for a few days."

"May I see him?"

"For a few minutes," the doctor said. She gestured to a nurse. "He's sleeping."

* * *

I think my mother was hoping that my father would wake up while she was there. I think she would have loved to see him grin, even though normally his grin-ning drove her crazy. She said it was something he did to convince you he was innocent or sincere when, in actual fact (she said), it made him look like he was hiding something.

He didn't wake up. I thought maybe my mother would want to stay until he did. She stood beside his bed, watching him intently, frowning, as if she were trying to decide something. Then she said, "Come on, Robyn. We'd better get home."

"But—"

"You heard what the doctor said. He's going to be okay."

"Yeah, but—"

"He's sleeping. He'll probably sleep all night."

"But, Mom—"

"You can come back tomorrow," she said.

Henri was waiting out in the hall. She asked if we

wanted a drive home. My mother said, no, she had her car. Henri said, "Are you sure you should be driving?"

My mother seemed surprised by the question. She said, "We're divorced, Henri," as if that had anything to do with it. Henri just nodded and said she was going to stick around and wait for Vern, if that was okay with my mother. My mother said, "Why wouldn't it be?"

She was quiet all the way home.

* * *

The phone rang almost as soon as we got home. My mother stared at it as if it were rattling like a snake poised to strike.

"Get that, will you, Robyn?" she said. Her voice sounded funny, as if she were holding her breath at the same time she was talking.

I held my breath, too, as I picked up the phone and said hello. Mostly I was thinking, don't let it be bad news about my father. I don't know what my mother was thinking.

"Oh, hi, Ted," I said when I heard the voice on the other end of the line. I grinned, as relieved as if a math test had just been cancelled. But my mother was shaking her head. She fumbled on the kitchen counter for a pen. She was still shaking her head and mouthed *I'm not here* as she scribbled on the back of an envelope. "Uh, no, she isn't here," I said. My mother held up the envelope: *Don't tell him about Mac.* "No, I don't, Ted," I said. "Sure. Sure, I'll tell her." I hung up and looked at my mother. "He said to ask you to call him when you get a chance," I said.

"I'll make us something to eat," my mother said. "I don't know about you, but I didn't have any lunch. And look at the time."

It was after six. I followed her into the kitchen and watched her stare into the fridge. I can't be sure, but food didn't appear to be the number one thing on her mind.

"How about grilled cheese sandwiches?" she said.

I said, sure. Then I said, "Are you going to marry Ted?"

My mother set down the block of cheddar cheese she was holding and reached for a loaf of bread. She dug a frying pan out of the cupboard before she said, "Why are you asking?"

"He told me he proposed to you."

"He told you that? When? Just now?"

"I talked to him the other day."

"Oh." She started slicing cheese and setting the slices on pieces of bread.

"He said you won't take his calls. He looked hurt."

"Robyn, it's really none of your business what—" She stopped and looked at me. "Well, I guess that's not true." Her voice was softer now. "His proposal took me by surprise."

I waited.

"He's a sweet man," she said.

"Do you love him?"

She cut a few more slices of cheese. "I don't know," she said. "I just don't know." She was silent for a few moments. Then she said, "Where were you today, Robyn?"

Oh boy. I had been hoping she'd let that one go.

"You were grounded, you know. You were supposed to be cleaning out the garage."

I thought about the trick Mr. Hanover had played on me and how that had probably been my father's idea. I thought about how my mother would react if I told her about it and if I told her that I had been helping my father find Trisha. She would not be pleased.

"I was with Nick," I said. At least it was the truth.

"Oh." My mother had a lot of what she called "reservations" about me spending time with Nick. "When I called you that first time—"

"I was downtown."

She didn't look angry so much as disappointed. "You lied to me, Robyn."

"I'm sorry."

"You know, I'm not sure it's such a good idea—" She stopped, sighed, and then tried again. "Robyn, that boy . . ."

"I like him, Mom."

She peered deep into my eyes. "Robyn, there are so many *nice* boys around." She shook her head. "Is that where you were on Thursday night after you left your father's? With Nick?"

"No," I said. But I could tell she didn't believe me.

"If you want me to trust you, Robyn, you have to be honest with me."

"I am being honest," I said. She looked dubious. "I'm being honest about Thursday night. After I left Dad's place, I went to the high school where Ted was coaching. If you don't believe me, you can ask him. He drove me home."

She weighed this and must have decided that I was telling the truth. "You're supposed to be grounded for the weekend," she said. "But I know you'll want to see your father tomorrow. You can go to the hospital after you finish the garage."

"What about you?" I said. "Aren't you going, too?"

"I have work to do."

"But Dad—"

"It's a big case, Robyn. I have to be prepared."

Boy, she could be so cold sometimes. Still, after we ate — in silence — she called the hospital. She told me what a nurse had told her — that my father was sleeping, that his vital signs were good, his condition was stable — then she went to the den to work.

The phone rang. I answered it. It was Nick.

"I didn't know," I said.

Silence.

"Nick, I swear. I didn't know what was in that envelope. I didn't know what Trisha's father was going to do."

"I believe you," he said. "But what about your dad?"

"What about him?"

"Mr. Hanover got that tracking device from somewhere. Was it from your father? Did he know what was going to happen?"

I said I didn't know. I didn't tell him that I sure had my suspicions.

"Didn't you ask him?"

I told him what had happened.

"Wow," Nick said. "Is he going to be okay?"

"The doctor says he is. Nick, did you see Beej? Has she calmed down?"

"She was still pretty worked up when I left her," Nick said. He was quiet for a moment. Then he said, "She didn't look angry, Robyn. Did you notice that?"

"She looked angry enough to me. She slapped me."

"I don't mean Beej. I mean Trisha. When her stepfather showed up, she didn't look like she was mad at him, you know, like, get lost, I don't want to see you. She looked scared. Did you notice that?"

I hadn't. I had been too stunned by what had happened. I had seen the fury on Beej's face and the anger and disappointment on Nick's. But I hadn't especially noticed how Trisha looked, except that, for just a moment before she'd been led out of the room, her expression had changed. I tried to remember her face.

"She sounded scared, too," Nick said.

"Her stepfather says she's a real drama queen," I told him. "The first time she ran away and the police brought her home, she made all kinds of crazy accusations about him and her mother."

"Well, if that was an act, she sure had me convinced. If you ask me, that girl was scared of something and I think it was something more than the possibility that she was going to be grounded."

"She fights with her mother a lot . . . and I guess she doesn't like her stepfather much right now."

"I didn't like my stepfather, either," Nick said.

"And some days he scared me good. On those days, I bet I looked just like Trisha did today. Maybe we should check on her."

"Come on, Nick. It's over. She's home. She's with her mother who needs her."

"Maybe," Nick said. He didn't sound convinced.

I was tired of thinking about Trisha Carnegie. I hadn't wanted to get involved in the first place, but I'd been sucked in because I thought it was my fault she had run away. Now it was my fault — sort of — that she was home again when she didn't want to be. Still (I told myself) her mother needed her — now more than ever.

"I have a day pass for tomorrow. You know, so I can spend some time with my aunt."

"Oh?"

"So meet me, okay?"

"I can't. I'm grounded. I'm supposed to clean out the garage. The only time I'm allowed out is to go and see my father in the hospital."

"When?"

"What?"

"When are you going to see your dad?"

"Why?"

"I'll meet you."

"But—"

"I want to see you, Robyn. Okay?"

I said okay. I told him which hospital my father was in and when I thought I could get there. After he hung up, I put my make-up-with-Mom plan into action.

Chapter Fourteen

My mother was standing at the kitchen counter drinking a cup of coffee and looking professional in a tailored suit when I got up the next morning.

"I've got to run," she said.

"Me, too," I said.

She arched an eyebrow. "The garage," she said.

"Done."

"Done?"

"Last night." It had taken me until nearly two in the morning, but I'd finished the job.

My mother carried her coffee mug down the three steps at the back of the kitchen to the door that led to the garage. She opened it. Then she looked back up at me.

"Okay," she said. "You're ungrounded."

"Have a nice day, Mom."

* * *

I went to the hospital first. Vern was there, sitting on a chair in the corner of the room. He got up when I entered the room and steered me back into the hall.

"He's still sleeping," he said. "He woke up for a few minutes last night."

"Did he say what happened?"

"Some guys jumped him. That's all he knows. The cops don't have anything yet." He glanced back over his shoulder. "He's probably going to sleep most of the day. I was planning to stick around." He glanced up and down the hallway. "Is your mother here with you?"

I shook my head. "Vern? Did Dad say anything to you about Trisha?"

"The Hanover girl? You mean, recently? No. Why?"

"Just wondering."

I tiptoed back into the room and kissed my father on the cheek. I told Vern I'd be back.

* * *

Nick wasn't at the park near the hospital when I got there. He wasn't there nearly a half hour later, either. I was beginning to think that he had stood me up when I finally spotted him. He had Beej by one hand, and she was straining in the opposite direction, as if she didn't want to be anywhere near him. Then she looked past him to me and our eyes met. Correction: she didn't want to be anywhere near *me*.

She pulled harder in the opposite direction until Nick stopped, turned to face her, and caught hold of her other hand, too. He said something to her. She shook her head. He said something else. She shook her head more vehemently. Nick stood perfectly still.

He said something else and then let go of both her hands.

Beej stayed where she was. She and Nick looked at each other for a few moments longer and then Nick said something else. He nodded in my direction. Beej looked at me again, still not smiling, still giving the impression that I was the last person on the planet she wanted to see, let alone talk to. But she straightened her shoulders, adjusted the battered backpack she was wearing, and together they walked toward me.

"Sorry I'm late," Nick said. Beej didn't say anything. Nick nudged her toward a picnic table. She sat down and glared at me, as if it were my fault she was here.

"Go on," Nick said. "Tell Robyn what you told me."

Beej looked sullenly at me.

"I don't get it," she said. "Why do you even care? The way Trisha tells it, you always treated her bad."

Always? Except for the history assignment, I'd never treated her any way at all. I'd barely had anything to do with her. I thought she was weird . . . Oh. Maybe that's what she meant.

"Back at that abandoned building, you said you and Trisha weren't friends," I said. "So why were you helping her?"

Beej's eyes shifted away from mine. She shrugged. "She was scared. She needed a place to hide. She promised to pay me. She said her mother is rich. She showed me a picture of her house. It's big." She looked at me. "It's for real, right?"

"Yeah, it's for real," I said. "But what do you mean, she needed a place to hide? From who? And what was she scared of?"

"From her stepfather," Beej said, as if this were obvious. "She's afraid of him."

"Afraid of him?" I glanced at Nick. "But he told my father that she always runs away after arguments with her mother. He thinks that's why she took off this time, because her mother is sick and Trisha can't deal with it."

"Well, he's lying," Beej said, sounding delighted to be correcting me. "She ran away because of her stepfather. She hates him *and* she's afraid of him. She said he was a horrible person. And she's worried about her mother. She has this piece of crystal that she was always meditating with. She said her mother was sick and she was afraid she wouldn't get better. Then she'd be stuck with Carl. Carl's the reason she took off. Not her mother. And she didn't just run away the way some kids do. She was so scared of him that she took off without any planning."

"What do you mean?"

"I mean, she left home empty-handed," Beej said. "No clothes, no cash, nothing. When I met up with her, all she had was the clothes she was wearing. She showed me her bank card, but she was afraid to use it. She said if she did, Carl could get an idea of where she was. I offered to use it for her — you know, get some money for her — but she said no, the banks have cameras everywhere and all that would happen is Carl would know who was helping her. But she promised me that as soon as her mother got better, she'd pay me."

I hated to be the one to tell her, but, "Her mother may not get better," I said.

Beej slapped her thigh. "Oh great! I bet that means I won't get paid. And how am I supposed to get my camera back?"

That's when I said something stupid. I said, "*You* have a camera?"

"Of course I have a camera," Beej said, indignant. "How do you think I took those pictures I had when I met you?" She looked at Nick and said, "That's it. I'm out of here."

"Robyn didn't mean that the way it sounded," he said. "She hasn't been around much, you know?"

"No kidding," Beej said. She turned on me. "You think because I don't live at home, I'm some pathetic loser who doesn't have anything?" she said. "Yeah, I have a camera. As a matter of fact, I have *two* — a still camera *and* a video camera."

"Beej takes great pictures," Nick said. "There was a project at the youth centre last year — a street art program. Beej's pictures were part of it. She even sold a couple."

I looked at her, at her fierce eyes, her wild hair and her pierced eyebrow, and decided maybe there was more to her than I had thought.

"Beej has been working on a video," Nick said.

She dug into her backpack, pulled out a videocassette, and slapped it onto the picnic table. "This," she said, "is gonna be great — *if* I ever finish it. Which is now a gigantic *if*, thanks to you." She glowered at me again. "Trisha has my video camera. It's one of those new ones, you know, compact. You have any idea how many flyers I had to deliver, how many flowers I had to pack, to pay for that camera?"

I glanced at Nick. His expression said, *Don't ask.*

"I should never have listened to Kenny," Beej said.

"Kenny Merchant?"

"He said, if you help her, she'll definitely pay you. Now it looks like I'm not going to get paid, *and* she still has my video camera. She borrowed it — without asking. She had it in her bag when Carl grabbed her."

No wonder Beej had kept grabbing at Trisha's bag.

"I also talked to Kenny," Nick said.

"You did?" I said. "When?"

"Last night." He looked at Beej. "Kenny told me that Trisha's scared but that she wouldn't tell him why. She said, the less he knew, the safer he'd be."

Beej looked mildly surprised. "She told me the same thing," she said. "Right after she called home."

"*What?*"

"She told me the same thing—"

"Trisha called home?" I said. Mr. Hanover had told my father and me that, unlike all the other times she had run away, Trisha hadn't called home.

"Sure, she called," Beej said. "She called to talk to her mother. But Carl answered and he told her he'd come and get her if she wanted, but he wouldn't put her through to her mother."

"When did she phone home?" I said.

"The day Kenny brought her to my place. Thursday." The day after Trisha had run. "I was there when she made the call, watching her back. I heard her beg her stepfather. She said all she wanted to do was talk to her mother. And every time she called after that, the call went straight through to voice mail. Trisha left messages, but I bet you anything Carl erased all of those calls before Trisha's mother could hear them. That's why Trisha wanted the letter. She wanted to know if her mother was okay."

"What do you mean, you were watching her back?"

"You know, making sure no one grabbed her."

"Grabbed her?"

"She was afraid to go out during the day," Beej said. "She acted like she was terrified of Carl. On the phone, she promised him she wouldn't say anything if he left her mother alone."

Maybe Nick was right. Trisha wasn't just being stubborn and spiteful. She was afraid — *really* afraid.

"I believed her and didn't believe her, you know?" Beej said. "She's a little psycho. And the whole bank card thing? I thought that was a scam. I thought she didn't want to use it and she didn't want me to use it because she never planned to pay me. That whole thing about Carl being able to find her if she used it—"

"She was right about that," I said.

Beej snorted. "Yeah, right."

"The banks can tell when a card was used and where. They have cameras on all their cash machines, so they can see who used it. The cops or someone with good contacts" — like my father — "would have seen it was you. Then they'd have started looking for you, too. It would have doubled their chances of finding Trisha."

Beej eyed me suspiciously. "And you know this because—"

"My father used to be a cop."

Beej gave Nick a sharp look. Nick shrugged apologetically.

"Did she say anything else to you about her stepfather or why she was afraid?" I said.

"She said if she was found, she'd probably be killed."

"*What?*" I said.

Beej looked almost apologetic. "I'm just telling you what she said. Like I told you, I didn't believe her. I thought she was, you know—"

"Psycho?" Nick said.

"Half the kids on the street, they're spinning stories about why they're there. Most of it isn't true."

"Yeah," Nick said grimly. "Most of it's worse than they say. Did she tell you anything else?"

Beej shook her head. A split-second later she half-nodded. "She said something about dead horses." She pondered this. "Yeah. She said she never liked her stepfather, but she never thought he'd be such a rat, letting someone get away with killing animals. Killing horses."

My heart slammed to a stop. I felt weak in the knees as I looked at Nick. I said, "Maybe you're right. Maybe we should check on Trisha."

Chapter Fifteen

Nick jogged back to where Beej and I were standing, on the corner of the street where Trisha lived.

"Well?" I said.

Nick shook his head. "There's a car pulled up at the side of the house. You can't see it from the street, though. I had to sneak up and peek through some bushes. And the people next door? They have a couple of Rottweilers that could use some basic training. Those guys would have ripped me apart if they could have got at me."

"Maybe that's what they've been trained for," Beej said. "Wow, look at the size of these houses!" She gazed around in awe.

"What about Trisha?" I said.

"I didn't see her," Nick said. "I didn't see anyone. Just the car with the trunk open. A suitcase in it. And a box of stuff — it looked like books and pictures. Personal stuff. Girl stuff. Looks like maybe someone is taking a trip."

"Trisha's mother is in the hospital," I said. "So why would Trisha or Mr. Hanover be going anywhere? Especially when he just brought Trisha home."

Nick shrugged. "Now what?" he said.

"I'm going to go and see if I can talk to Trisha," I said.

"Great," Beej said. "Come on. Let's go."

"You can't come with me," I told her. *Again.* I'd told her the same thing while Nick was checking out the house, not that she had listened. "Explain it to her, Nick."

"I don't need Nick to explain anything to me," she said. "It's not Nick's video camera. It's mine. And I want it back."

"Beej," I said, as patiently as I could manage, "Mr. Hanover *knows* you helped Trisha. Someone followed you while you were leading Nick to where she was hiding. So it makes sense that if Trisha told anyone one of her so-called wild stories, it would have been you. He also saw you *slap* me, which means he's not going to think you told *me* anything. But if you go up to the house with me, he might get suspicious and think you told me whatever Trisha told you. He might also think you know something — and that could be dangerous for you." Well, it could be — assuming that there was anything to tell. Assuming the dead horses Trisha had mentioned to Beej were the same dead horses I suspected they were.

"She's right, Beej," Nick said.

Beej gave him a look that made it clear that he had lost all credibility with her, thanks one hundred percent to his association with me.

"Can you at least ask her about my video camera?" she said.

"If I see her, I'll ask. I promise."

"Maybe we should just call the cops," Nick said.

"And tell them what?" I said. "That Trisha Carnegie is finally back home?"

"Tell them what we know — that she told Beej she was afraid for her life."

"I don't know if it's true, but according to Carl, Trisha has made all kinds of crazy accusations about her parents to the police. They probably won't believe us — not unless there's some evidence."

Nick shook his head. "Okay," he said reluctantly. "We'll wait for you here." He had already scouted the area for the nearest pay phone. "If you're not back in fifteen minutes, I'm calling you on your cell phone. If you don't answer" — he broke off and looked lost for a moment, as if he wasn't sure what he'd do. I pulled out a pen and a piece of paper — actually, a bus transfer — from my purse and scribbled a phone number on it.

"If I don't come back, call Vern," I said. "He's my dad's partner. Tell him exactly what's going on. He'll know what to do."

Nick looked relieved to have a backup plan that could actually work.

"It's going to be okay," I told him. "All I'm going to do is ask to see Trisha."

"And find out about my video camera," Beej said. "Don't forget."

Carl Hanover opened the door at about the time that I started thinking that maybe this wasn't such a good idea after all. Suppose Nick was right? Suppose Trisha had been afraid — and for a good reason? Suppose my father's old friend Carl Hanover wasn't a nice man? Suppose the dead horses Trisha had mentioned really were the horses that had died at the Doig place? The insurance company Mr. Hanover worked for had paid out a lot of money for those horses. Suppose . . .

And then there he was, smiling down at me, looking relaxed and healthy with his nice deep tan.

"Robyn, hello," he said. "I heard about your father. What happened? How is he?"

"They're not sure what happened," I said. "But he's going to be fine."

I edged toward the door, the way you do when you're expecting someone to invite you in. Mr. Hanover shifted a little so that he was blocking the way almost completely. I peeked around him into the house, but all I could see was the spacious foyer. One door off it led to a dining room, another to a vast living room. Behind him, a staircase wound up to the second floor. A long narrow table stood along one wall. Beside the table was a cardboard box with some clothes in it that could only be Trisha's. On the table were a phone, a lamp, a flower arrangement — I couldn't tell whether it was fresh or artificial. Beside the arrangement was Trisha's D&G backpack (gaping open so that something square and black was clearly visible inside — if Beej were here, she would have tackled Mr. Hanover to the ground to get at it) — and something else. Something that convinced me that Nick had been right.

"Well, I'm glad to hear that," Mr. Hanover said. "I bet he thought he'd left that sort of thing behind when he left the police force."

"I guess," I said. "Mr. Hanover, about Trisha—"

"I'm sorry I had to trick you, Robyn," he said. "I didn't know what I'd do if I didn't get her home. I didn't know what her mother would do."

His expression seemed sincere and he looked sad when he mentioned his wife. But if he cared so much for her, why hadn't he let Trisha talk to her when she called home? And why had he told my father and me that he hadn't heard from her at all?

"That's okay," I said. "I understand. I don't think those kids who delivered that letter will ever talk to me again. But I'm glad Trisha's home and everything is okay."

"It wouldn't have happened without your help, Robyn," he said. "Thank you for everything." He took a step back inside, getting ready to close the door.

"I was wondering if I could see her," I said.

He looked surprised.

"She's in one of my classes," I said. "And—" I looked suitably contrite. "I said something to her the last time I saw her in school. Something I regret. I'd like to apologize."

"Ah," he said. "Well, Trisha isn't here at the moment. Her mother is very ill." His eyes went to the floor for a moment. When he looked up again, they were filled with tears. "I'm sorry," he said. "It's just all the pressure with Trisha missing and now Denise—"

I looked back around him to the table near the stairs — at Trisha's bag, and beside it, the chain from which hung her father's wedding ring and the little pouch that held her meditating crystal. The chain that she supposedly *always* wore. If the stories I had heard about Trisha were true, then I couldn't imagine Trisha taking it off, much less leaving it lying around, after what had happened. She had told Kenny Merchant and Beej that she hated Mr. Hanover. Supposedly that was the reason she always wore that ring — to remind him of that.

"Do you know when she's going to be back?" I said. "Because I'd really like—"

"She went to the hospital to see her mother," he said. "I was just on the way there myself. But I'll tell her you were here, okay?"

I said okay, even though it didn't feel okay.

As I headed back down the walk, I heard dogs barking. It was probably the Rottweilers next door that Nick had told me about. Then I heard a *thunk* that sounded exactly like the trunk of a car being slammed shut. I glanced back at the house and saw Mr. Hanover standing at the window, watching me. He was not smiling anymore. Nor did he look anything like Nice Mr. Hanover or Worried Mr. Hanover or Dutiful Husband Mr. Hanover. I waved as I left the property.

"Well?" Nick said.

"He says she's not there."

"I knew it," Beej said. "I knew it. I'll never get my video camera back."

"I saw it," I said.

"You did?" If I hadn't grabbed her by the arm, she would have raced up to the house to reclaim it. "I gotta get my camera back," she said. She strained against me. I think she might have hit me if Nick hadn't stepped in.

"You think he's lying?" he said.

That caught Beej's attention. She turned back toward me. I nodded.

"Tell me again about the dead horses," I said to Beej. "What exactly did she say?"

"Just what I told you — that her stepfather is a creep and she never liked him, but she never realized that he could be so evil. And how if her mother could see the truth, how the guy's really a creep, she'd be out of there in a flash."

"Robyn, what's going on?" Nick said.

"What do you think she was doing with your video camera?" I said.

"How do I know?" Beej said. "What do people usually do with a video camera?"

Nick looked at me. "Make videos," he said slowly. "Do you think Trisha made a video?"

"The day Trisha ran away, she left school to go home to get something she forgot," I said. At least, I was pretty sure that's what she had done. She had looked horrified when she'd discovered that her work wasn't in her backpack. She had collided with Angry Alison on her way out of school. I would have bet anything she was going home to get it. "The day before that, Howie Maritz died." Nick shook his head. He had no idea who I was talking about. "He was a fire marshal," I said. "He investigated the fire at that stable back in the summer, the one where all those horses died."

"But what does that have to do with Trisha?" Nick asked.

"Mr. Hanover works for an insurance company — the same insurance company that insured the stable where the fire happened."

"You think he had something to do with the fire?" Nick said.

"I don't know. But Trisha said that her stepfather had talked about dead horses. It's kind of a big coincidence, don't you think? The insurance company he works for paid a lot of money after the fire, but only *after* the fire marshal said the fire was accidental and *after* someone at Mr. Hanover's insurance company looked at the claim. The fire marshal died the day before Trisha ran away. Supposedly it was a suicide."

"Supposedly?" Beej said.

"The next day, the day after the suicide, Trisha left school and she never came back. She ran away, and after that she was scared, really scared, to go back home. She told you she was afraid someone was going to kill her. She talked about someone killing horses. And, Nick, you said yourself that she looked terrified when her stepfather grabbed her. Now Mr. Hanover is saying she isn't in the house. But her purse is there and so is the ring that she always — and I mean *always* — wears around her neck. I saw some of her stuff in a box in the hall. Mr. Hanover said she's at the hospital with her mother, but if the stories I've heard about Trisha are true, she wouldn't go anywhere without her father's ring. Mr. Hanover said he was just on his way to the hospital, too, but you saw a suitcase and a bunch of girl stuff in the trunk of the car."

"What are you saying, Robyn?"

"I'm saying I think maybe Trisha is going to run away again, only this time I think she's going to disappear for good."

"What?" Nick said.

"I think she knows something about those horses. Maybe when she went home that day, she heard something or saw something she shouldn't have. Maybe she was afraid to go to the police because of her mother. Maybe she was afraid something might happen to her mother if she did."

It was starting to make sense. I remembered what Trisha had said when those two men with her stepfather had grabbed her. She had asked him what he had done to her mother. What if Mr. Hanover had been using his wife to threaten Trisha? What if he had told Trisha that something bad would happen to her mother if she said anything to the police?

"If Trisha's mother is as sick as Mr. Hanover says she is, he won't be able to use her to keep Trisha quiet for much longer. That's why he was so desperate to find her. That's why he tricked me. If Trisha's mother died, Trisha wouldn't be afraid to go to the police anymore."

"Do you think her stepfather is going to hurt her?" Nick said.

I thought about what had just happened. At the same time that I had heard the sound of the trunk closing around the side of the house, I had seen Mr. Hanover watching me from the window at the front of the house. That meant that someone besides Mr. Hanover had closed that trunk.

"I think that's exactly what Mr. Hanover and his friends are planning," I said. "I don't think he's alone, Nick. I think those same two guys are with him. And if they leave here with Trisha—"

"Maybe now would be a good time to call the cops," Nick said.

"And tell them what?" Beej said. "That we're afraid someone *might* do something to Trisha? And, anyway, how fast would they get here, assuming you could even get them to come?"

"I think Nick's right," I said. "I think we should call the cops. And we have to find a way to keep Mr. Hanover here until they arrive."

"How do you suggest we do that?" Beej said. "Form a human chain in front of the driveway?"

"Trisha borrowed your video camera," I said. "Maybe she was planning to make a video about what she saw or heard — you know, in case anything happened to her or her mother."

"But we don't know for sure that she did make a video. And even if she did, we don't know where it is," Nick said.

"Neither does Mr. Hanover," I said. "But he does know that she had access to a video camera. It's right there in her bag. What would he do if he thought she had made a video? What if he thought that *we* had that video?"

"But we don't."

Nick eyed me closely. "What are you going to do, Robyn?"

I turned to Beej. "You have a videocassette in your bag, right?"

"Yeah," she said hesitantly.

"Can I see it?"

"It's my project—"

"I just want to borrow it."

"Robyn—" Nick said.

I opened my bag and took out my cell phone. "Call 911," I said. "Then call Vern and tell him what's going on."

"If you're right and this guy is dangerous—"

"Tell them at 911 that you heard screams and a gunshot," I said. "Just do it, Nick." I turned to Beej. "You want your video camera back?"

"You have to ask?" She slung off her backpack and crouched down to burrow into it. She pulled out an envelope of pictures, then a camera and then — ta-da! — the videocassette. "I'll hang onto it, okay?"

"But if we're calling 911—" Nick said.

"We have to stop him from leaving with Trisha," I

said. I looked down at Beej's other camera, the still camera. "You have film in that?"

Beej rolled her eyes. "It's digital," she said.

"Call them now, Nick," I said.

Chapter Sixteen

Trisha was in Mr. Hanover's arms. Her eyes were closed. Her head lolled against his chest. Her arms and legs dangled as limply as a rag doll's. I glanced at Beej, who hung back near the entrance to the driveway. She raised her camera and snapped a picture before Mr. Hanover even noticed. Another man came out of the door behind Mr. Hanover. I recognized him immediately. The man with the mirrored aviator glasses, the man who had followed me. When he spotted me and Beej, he said, "Hey!" and raised his hand in front of his face the way movie stars do when they're being accosted by paparazzi. "Hey!" he said again, and Mr. Hanover turned his head. Unlike the big man in the aviator sunglasses, Mr. Hanover didn't look angry. He looked stunned.

"Poor Trisha," he said, nodding at her, still limp in his arms. "She isn't feeling well."

With a little help from her friends, I thought. Then I thought, how fast *is* police response time?

"I'm taking her to the doctor," Mr. Hanover said. "With her mother so sick, it's all been too much for her."

The man in the sunglasses nodded, but there was nothing in that curt gesture that suggested agreement. Then I saw who he was nodding to. Another man, a big, bouncer-sized man whom I had also seen, back at the abandoned building where Trisha had been hiding. Mr. Hanover saw him, too, and looked worried.

"Dan," he said. Boy, and it sounded like a warning. A *scared* warning.

I stood very quietly for a moment, listening for police sirens in the distance and hearing instead the pounding of my heart in my chest. Then, because there didn't seem to be any alternative, I said, "The thing is, Mr. Hanover, Trisha made a videotape."

Mr. Hanover understood immediately, but the man in the aviator sunglasses didn't. He frowned and looked at Mr. Hanover.

"You saw the video camera in her bag," I said. "I know you did."

The man in the aviator sunglasses scowled. "What's she talking about, Carl?"

"We have the videotape," I said. I nodded to Beej. Out of the corner of my eye I saw her, way back behind me, holding up the videocassette so that Mr. Hanover could see it. "She videotaped the whole story," I said. "She told everything she knows." Whatever that was.

The man in the sunglasses reached inside his jacket.

Behind me I heard Beej say, "Smile!" She was pointing her digital camera at the man.

"Hey!" the man said again, his hand coming out of his jacket and, geeze, there it was, a gun.

"Say cheese," Beej said, aiming her camera again.

"Hey!" The man turned his head now.

"Again," Beej said.

"Grab her!" the man said to his partner, Bouncer Boy.

"You," the man said, pointing his gun at me.

"Cheese," Beej said.

The man grew even more flustered now, but not because of Beej and her camera. He heard a sound in the distance — we all heard it. It was a pulsing sound and it was slowly getting louder.

Sirens.

Then there was a blur of activity. The other man, Bouncer Boy, thundering past me. Me turning and seeing that Beej wasn't there anymore. The guy in the sunglasses swearing, over and over, then moving toward the car and jumping into it while Mr. Hanover just stood there: a statue of a man with a rag doll girl in his arms.

While sirens pulsed closer and closer.

Then there were police officers advancing on the place. Blocking the driveway.

Then there was Nick.

And Beej, talking to a cop a mile a minute.

While Mr. Hanover stood exactly where he was, looking pale under his nice tan.

Chapter Seventeen

For a guy with a ruptured spleen — which turned out to have been a minor rupture — a couple of cracked ribs and a monster headache, my father looked exceptionally happy. Possibly it was because the case he had been working on had reached a conclusion.

People were talking, and it now looked as if the horse trainer who had died was a victim of arson; he had died because Carmine Doig had needed ready cash more than he needed well-insured horses. The fire marshal's suicide was now looking like murder — apparently he'd had second thoughts about ruling the fire accidental. He'd been planning to go to the police. Trevor Bailey, the claims adjuster who had signed the report, talked to the police. He told them that he hadn't done the actual investigation. Carl Hanover had handled that. Then, using his wife's illness as an excuse to take a leave from work, he had asked Trevor Bailey to handle the last-minute details and sign the report. That way, his name didn't appear on the official record. Carl Hanover was arrested on conspiracy to commit fraud. He said he'd gone along with Doig's plan because he was being blackmailed. My father said if that was true, maybe he could make a deal with the prosecutor. Of course, there was still the matter of what he and his blackmailers had been planning to do to Trisha.

Or possibly my father looked happy because, as he had said over and over again, he was proud of me. Okay, so I shouldn't have confronted Mr. Hanover the way I had — I think he scolded me about it partly to pacify my mother — but still, "Good thinking, Robbie. *Brilliant* thinking. You probably saved that girl's life."

Mostly, though, I think he was so happy because sitting in the hospital with Vern and me was my mother. Nobody had forced her to come. Nor had she come because she was angry — she wasn't. She had arrived at the police station shortly after the police had taken us all there to make statements. Vern had called her. She had stayed by my side while I told my story (and Beej, in another room, told hers, and Nick, in another room, told his). Trisha had been taken to the hospital to recover from whatever her stepfather had drugged her with.

After we had finished with the police, my mother said, "We'd better go and tell Mac what's going on." By the time we got there, Vern had already briefed my father. And there he was, grinning. Mom looked calm and pleased to see he was recovering. We were a pretty happy group.

"I'd sure like to talk to Trisha," I said.

My father glanced at Vern.

"She was released from here an hour ago, but you'll probably find her at St. Mary's," Vern said. "That's where her mother is."

St. Mary's specialized in cancer treatments.

"I can drive you," my mother said.

I accepted her offer.

I bought some flowers in the hospital gift shop and took them with me upstairs to the room where Trisha's mother was. Through the open door, I could see Trisha sitting by her mother's bedside. She looked pale and tired. She got up when she saw me and thanked me for the flowers, which she set on a table near her mother's bed. Then she came out into the hall.

"I wanted to apologize," I said. "I'm sorry for what I said at school, and I'm really sorry for leading your stepfather to you."

"It's okay," Trisha said. "You didn't know. And the police said you saved my life."

I glanced into the room behind her.

"How is your mother?"

Trisha moved away from the door. Her voice was quiet but strong when she said, "Not good. But you don't know my mom. She's a fighter. She's not going to give up and neither am I."

For the first time ever, I actually admired Trisha. She seemed so determined.

"What happened that day, Trisha?" I said. "The day you left school."

"I went home to get the work I had done. I really

did do it, Robyn," she said. "I know you think I didn't, but I did. It's just with my mom . . ."

"I believe you," I said.

"I let myself into the house and Carl was there. I heard him talking to a man he called Carmine. There was another man with him — he was really creepy. He was the guy who found me at Beej's place."

The man with the aviator sunglasses.

"The man named Carmine was reminding Carl that what had happened to the fire marshal could easily happen to him." She looked at me. "The night before I was in my mom's room with her. We were watching the news together. We always do. I like to keep her company, you know? There was an item about the fire marshal — it said he had committed suicide. Carl came into the room while it was on. You should have seen the look on his face when he heard that. He went white. The news also mentioned the fire at Carmine Doig's stable. And now Carl was talking to a man named Carmine, and Carmine was threatening him."

"The police say now that the fire marshal's death wasn't suicide," I said.

"I know," Trisha said. "Anyway, the guy with Carmine came out into the hall and saw me. He tried to grab me. So did Carl, but I got away from them. When I was running out the door, he said something about my mother. He said something would happen to her. But I ran anyway. Afterwards, I started to worry. What did he mean, something would happen to her? Was he going to hurt her?"

"Is that why you tried to call home?"

She nodded. "I phoned from a shopping mall. Carl wouldn't let me speak to her. He said if I didn't come home, he couldn't guarantee that those men wouldn't hurt her. He said they would hurt her for sure if I went to the police. I didn't know what to do. I didn't want him to find me, but I didn't want him to hurt my mother, either."

"Is that when you contacted Kenny?"

She nodded.

"He said he knew someone who could help me."

"Beej."

"Yeah. And I tried to call home again. But Carl still wouldn't let me talk to my mother. He told me to come home. He said, 'You don't know what kind of people these are, Trisha. But if you come home, I think I could convince them not to hurt you.' I didn't believe him, so I made a videotape, just in case anything happened to me or my mother. I wasn't going to let them get away with it."

"Where is the tape?"

"Kenny has it. I told him that if anything happened, he should give it to the police."

"I heard that your stepfather is blaming it all on Carmine Doig and his people," I said. "He says Doig was blackmailing him and that it was Doig's idea to make it look like you ran away for good. They were going to say you took off because you thought your mother . . ." I couldn't make myself say the words. "I'm glad it worked out, Trisha," I said. "I hope your mother gets better."

"Thanks, Robyn," she said. "Me, too."

When I went to see my father again, he was sitting up in bed and looking a lot better. I told him what Trisha had told me. But there was one thing I didn't understand.

"Who attacked you, Dad? Did it have anything to do with Carmine Doig and Trisha?"

My father nodded. He said he'd received a call promising him information. He had been able to describe one of the men who'd attacked him to Detective Sergeant Harwood, who had produced a photo array. The man my father had identified worked for Carmine Doig. I went pale when I realized how close my father had come to—

"It's okay, Robbie," my father said. He squeezed my hand. "I'm fine."

It took me a while to get rid of the scared, shaky feeling. I kept thinking, what if that security guard hadn't come along when he did? Would those men have killed my father?

"Robbie, really, I'm okay," my father said.

I had one more question. I almost didn't want to ask it, but I needed to know.

"Dad, did you tell Mr. Hanover to trick me?"

The question seemed to hurt my father.

"You went outside in the hall to talk to him the last time he was at your place," I reminded him. "The next thing I knew, he handed me a letter with a tracking device in it."

"He told me he had the feeling you weren't being completely honest," my father said. He paused to look at me, until I felt my cheeks flush. "He said Denise was frantic to get a message to Trisha. I told him I trusted you, Robbie. I didn't like the way he approached you with that letter, and I told him so. He apologized. I should have thought more about it at the time."

"I should have told you about Kenny," I said.

He looked hard at me. "I'm sure you had your reasons not to," he said. "You're old enough to make your own decisions. You're also old enough to live with the consequences."

He was right about that.

Chapter Eighteen

I sat in my mother's car at the curb outside of my father's building.

"Are you *sure* you don't mind?" I said.

"Robyn, for heaven's sake, you've asked me that a dozen times today. And a dozen and a half times yesterday. And the answer is still the same. No, I don't mind."

"But we've always spent my birthday together," I said. I felt bad about leaving her alone.

"Well, maybe it's time for a change," she said.

"You want to come upstairs and say hi to Dad?"

"I don't think so." She looked at me for a few moments. "When you and Nick go out tonight," she said, "your father's going to tell you, *Don't do anything I wouldn't do*. But, Robyn, that doesn't cover much territory. So do me a favour, okay? Don't do anything *I* wouldn't do."

I laughed and then, because she was serious, I promised.

"What are you going to do, Mom?"

"I'm going to go and see Ted."

Oh. "And?"

"And we're going to talk."

"Are you going to say yes?"

She shook her head slowly. "But I don't think I'm going to say no, either. I need time, Robyn."

"It's okay, Mom," I said. "I really like Ted. But I really love you."

She leaned over and kissed me. "Happy birthday, sweetie."

When I let myself into my father's loft, Nick was sitting on the couch looking nervous. My father looked amused. He engulfed me in as big a daddy bear hug as he could under the circumstances and said, "Happy birthday, Robbie." When he finally let me go, he pressed a small box into my hand. I opened it. It was my birthstone, set in gold on a gold chain, with matching earrings. I hugged him again.

Nick stood in the background. He was out of Somerset now and was staying with my father temporarily. He'd finally talked to someone at Somerset and he and his aunt were going to counselling. My father had told Nick, Don't worry. You can stay here as long as you want. He said, I can set you up in some space downstairs if it comes to that. Nick had looked so relieved. He didn't get breaks like this too often.

He looked terrific now in black pants, a purple-blue shirt that complemented his eyes, and a black jacket. It all looked brand new.

"I took him shopping," my father said. "You know, so Fred won't have a fit."

"Fred? Fred Smith?" The owner of La Folie.

"The other part of your present," my father said. "Anything on the menu. It's all taken care of."

I hugged him again. Then I turned to Nick, who smiled shyly at me.

"You okay?" I said.

"It's just that the place is so fancy," he said. "What if I used the wrong fork or something?"

"Just watch me," I said. I took his hand in mine.

"Have a good time, you two," my father said. "And Robbie? Don't do anything I wouldn't do." He winked at me.